5/80

F y

WESTE[...]

D0423322

D.day
'80
188

WINTER DRIFT

Also by Carter Travis Young

THE WILD BREED
SHADOW OF A GUN
THE SAVAGE PLAIN
THE BITTER IRON
LONG BOOTS, HARD BOOTS
WHY DID THEY KILL CHARLEY?
WINCHESTER QUARANTINE
THE POCKET HUNTERS
WINTER OF THE COUP
THE CAPTIVE
BLAINE'S LAW
GUNS OF DARKNESS
RED GRASS

Winter Drift

CARTER TRAVIS YOUNG

DOUBLEDAY & COMPANY, INC.

GARDEN CITY, NEW YORK

1980

First Edition

ISBN: 0-385-12327-2
Library of Congress Catalog Card Number 79-7886
Copyright © 1980 by Doubleday & Company, Inc.
All Rights Reserved
Printed in the United States of America

CHAPTER 1

~~~ 1 ~~~

It was late afternoon. The wind continued to blow from the north. The wind and the cold and the fresh powder snow that had been falling since morning. The blowing snow hung over the land like a white mist, clothing the gauntness of its bones like pale flesh.

Winter had come early to Texas that year. There had been snow in late November, and the cold had held. Most of the snow remained frozen on the ground, caught in white folds in the wagon ruts leading down the long slope toward the creek, piled high against the side of the shed and the wooden water trough and the lean-to shelter on the north side of the barn. The rocky hills to the north, which provided some shelter for the buildings clustered on a small shelf above the creek, wore great collars of snow like the purest sheep's wool. Even the sharp ax cut of the canyon out of which the creek meandered was blunted by the deep drifts.

Peering through the window, Trish Lovell wondered if she could have imagined the lone rider on the ridge to the northeast, stark against the lowering sky. She put her hand on the glass to wipe away the condensation, and shivered involuntarily at its cold touch. Dark was closing in early, the premature darkness of the storm, and she could no longer even make out the line of the ridge clearly.

But someone—something—had been there.

A lone rider out in this storm might be anyone. Not
likely a drifter; any such would have seen the storm coming and headed for shelter, seeking the warmth and company of the town of Cedar Point some twenty miles to
the east. An Indian, possibly. Or Ramon—this last
thought quickened hope—returning from wherever he
had gone.

Or—she shivered again, not with cold—it might be Virgil Pryor coming home.

She told herself that it was possible she had imagined
the rider. The snow and the failing light played tricks
with vision, especially when you stared out for a long
time, as she had taken to doing lately, half hoping that
she would see someone coming, half afraid that she
would.

It had been different when she knew that Pegleg Parks
and Ramon Sanudo were about the place. Then she had
not minded being alone in the house. She had even been
relieved when Pryor left, and as the days since his de-
parture stretched into weeks her relief had grown into a
quiet pleasure in her freedom. He had not told her where
he was going or how long he would be gone. That was
like him. Not only was he secretive about his actions, but
he also enjoyed having her know that she could never be
certain when he might suddenly reappear. She dared not
leave the house for long, knowing what would be in store
for her if he should happen to return and find her gone.

It was not jealousy that trapped her, although he sometimes acted and even talked as if it were. He simply
wanted her there when it was his pleasure, the way some
men wanted a woman to pet or to kick according to
whim.

He would be furious when he found her there alone.
Not even Pegleg would escape that rage, broken leg and
all. A gimpy, harmless old-timer whom Virgil Pryor kept

on at the ranch and worked ragged in exchange for beans in his belly and a leaking roof over his head, Pegleg had been crushed against a wall of the barn by the black-and-white pinto when the horse shied suddenly from a scurrying rat. The same thing might have happened a score of times without damage, but Pegleg's bones were old and brittle, or so it seemed. His right leg—the good one—had snapped below the knee. Over his protests Trish had struggled to load him into the wagon and had driven him into town to the doctor. That was five days ago, and she wondered when she would see him again. He had looked so small and forlorn when she had left him, his eyes filled with pain and fear, as if he felt that she was abandoning him. His face had been gray with the pain of his long, jouncing ride in the wagon.

Virgil Pryor would feel no sympathy; he would blame Pegleg for his carelessness.

As for Ramon, he had been gone a week, vanishing two days before Pegleg's accident. The sudden disappearance was not unusual, for the Mexican had done the same thing a number of times before in his silent, unpredictable way. But never when it meant that she would be left alone. If he didn't return before Pryor did, he would be better off never coming back, for he would face a killing rage.

After five days alone, Trish Lovell knew that she was quite capable of conjuring up ghosts on a ridge. She was frightened and lonely, with that sense of desolation she had known for too many of her twenty-two years. But she felt a deeper dread of Pryor's coming than of loneliness. Better a Comanche, she thought bitterly. But then the memory, buried deep but never covered over, of her close brush with death at the hands of Comanches snaked toward the surface of her mind, and she nearly cried out in sudden despair.

Almost immediately came revulsion at her weakness. She turned abruptly away from the window, which had clouded over from her breath as if receiving the silent imprint of her stifled cry, like an impression in sand carved by the wind. If the rider was real and not a ghost, she would be prepared to welcome him.

She moved quickly to lift the Winchester rifle from its pegs on the wall. She was a slender woman, almost slight, and the rifle looked huge in her hands, as if its weight might be too much for her to lift. In truth she was taller than she appeared, being about four inches above five feet in height, but her bones were small, as her mother's had been. (She no longer remembered her mother very clearly, but she recalled those words being spoken of her.) Her arms and wrists were thin, albeit surprisingly strong. Her figure had a woman's roundnesses, the breasts shapely under her plain homespun dress, but her waist was as narrow as a whisper and her hips were slim. Her legs, too, were slender—like sticks, she had often thought in moments of gloomy self-appraisal.

Her features were small and neat, the face somewhat long, the nose long and with a narrow bridge. It was a face familiar in the hill country of Tennessee, where she and her parents had lived before their fateful westward journey eight years ago. The only thing heavy about Trish Lovell was her hair, which was blond, thick and curly, the only feature in which she could find real pride, for she knew that it was beautiful.

It was her hair that had first caught Virgil Pryor's eye. He had liked to dig his hands into it, his strong fingers searching out the shape of her skull beneath the masses of curls.

She paused, giving her head a toss that produced a cascade of blond curls, remembering an occasion when Pryor had been less admiring of her hair. That time, with no one to see but Pegleg and Ramon, who dared not interfere, Pryor had dragged her by her hair clear across the yard, from the barn to the house, ignoring her cries of anguish, because she had not come as quickly as he wanted when he yelled at her.

He had wanted fresh coffee, that was all. The specific need was not what mattered to him. It was her instant obedience that he craved, and if his mood was surly in the morning he would command it with a cuff of his hand or with the humiliation and pain of dragging her across the ground like a bawling calf.

Her lips tight, Trish moved to the window. She was light of foot, and her steps made no sound on the bare wooden planks of the floor. The only sound in the house was the snap and spit of fresh wood burning in the fireplace, for she had recently built up the fire in preparation for cooking her evening meal as well as protection against the bone-deep chill of the approaching night. From outside there came no sound—she might have suspected the creature on the ridge of being a gray wolf prowling alone, if she had heard his howl; there had been nothing. And in any event the snow muffled all sound.

She wiped the window clean to peer out once more. A whirl of snow fled past the window like white dust, and cleared. And for an instant she was able to see the poles of the corral, laced with snow, and the bulky shape of the barn.

Something moved past the barn door, and she saw that it was open. She was certain that she had closed it when she checked the horses earlier. She would not have left it open to the snow and the cold wind.

Her heart thumped heavily, but her blood seemed to move with a strange sluggishness in her veins.

She backed away from the window and across the room. There she stood with her back against the wall, staring at the barred door, holding the rifle in her hands. Slowly she thumbed the hammer back and lifted the barrel until the muzzle pointed at the door.

A long minute passed, marked by the wild thudding of her heart. Her mind chased questions and fears. It was not Ramon. Rough and uncivilized as he sometimes seemed, often reminding her of an Indian, there was yet an odd courtliness about him toward her. Unfailingly he would call out if he knew that she was alone, hallooing to let her know she should not be concerned, that no savage had come to steal her beautiful hair. He would not come silently out of the storm's white wilderness to frighten her. As for Virgil Pryor, this stealthy coming was not his way either. It would have been more like him to ride straight up to the door of the house, expecting someone else to care for his horse while he stomped the snow from his boots in the warmth of the house.

She thought she heard a shuffling step outside and she went taut. The strain of holding and aiming the rifle was beginning to tell, and her hands shook. Her ears strained, listening for any call. But there was only the restless soughing of the wind, the crackling of the fire burning on the hearth, the blood beating in her ears like wings.

Pegleg! she thought suddenly. On crutches—that was why he had not hurried to the house to let her know he had returned. It must be him!

But almost as quickly as this hope came to her she knew that it was false. Doctor Hibbs had been concerned about the severity of that break in Pegleg's good leg. And with the other leg gimpy all along, there was no way Parks could have been back in the saddle so soon, fit to ride through a storm alone.

Besides, she realized with belated clarity, the figure on the ridge had been motionless, facing as if he were looking down at the house, studying it. No reason for Pegleg or Ramon or Virgil Pryor to do that. No reason for anyone but a stranger or a—

A heavy banging shuddered the door. In her anxious state Trish gasped involuntarily. Trembling, she stared at the door as if it were a thing alive, her finger on the trigger of the rifle. If he tried to break it down, she would shoot.

"Halloo! Anyone there?"

The unexpected sound of the voice startled her and, quite unpredictably, had the effect of calming her. She had been building up hysteria in her lonely, silent isolation, and the sound of another voice brought her abruptly back to a saner, more normal world. Hesitating, she lowered the rifle slightly.

Now she did hear a muted footstep. A hand appeared at the window, brushing snow aside, and a blurred face wavered behind the glass, indistinguishable, hardly more than a blob. She was not sure that he could see her through the mist on the window, but a moment later the pale blob disappeared and there was another knock on the door, softer this time—or perhaps it only seemed so because she was not as startled by it.

"Lookin' for the Pryor place. Would this be it?"

Trish found her voice at last. "Who are you? What do you want?" There was a quavery edge to her questions, for she had not yet gotten over her panic.

There was a momentary silence before the stranger said, "I'm lookin' to find a young woman, name of Patricia Lovell. Or maybe it's Patricia Pryor now."

Her jaw dropped in astonishment. Patricia! No one called her that anymore. No one had since she moved out of the Bauers' boardinghouse. Who could it be?

Surely not Henry Bauer after all this time; he wouldn't have the nerve.

She hesitated, but her fear was swiftly dissipating. She had conjured it up out of nothing but cabin fever. Still, anyone could have learned her name—and the stranger had not given his.

"I mean you no harm, ma'am," he said, so quietly that she could barely hear him.

Trish Lovell bit her lip. Perhaps she was being foolish, but she was thinking of the deep snow drifts, the cold and the blowing snow, and the swift approach of the long winter night. And she knew that she could not keep her door barred because of some nameless fear, refusing shelter from the storm to a stranger.

Slowly she approached the door. She had the rifle ready, and as she lifted the bar and called out, "Come in, then," she stepped quickly back out of reach.

The door pushed open. A tall man, his figure thickened by the snow piled on his bulky, sheepskin-lined jacket, stepped quickly into the room, ducking to clear the door-jamb with his head. A whirl of powder snow and a sharp fist of cold air struck through the doorway with him, and he quickly swung the door shut. Through this brief moment his face, wearing a frosty mustache and taut with cold, was offered to her for only an instant, yet something caused her heart to trip, and a vague sense of recognition tugged at her brain.

Then he turned and looked full at her.

For a long minute they stared at each other in silence. She thought she saw wonder grow in his gray eyes, eyes that were suddenly familiar to her, keenly remembered, known in her dreams long ago.

"You've growed," he said. "But I reckon I'd have known—"

"Oh my God!" she whispered. "It *is* you. . . ."

She felt her legs go soft at the knees. Her head swam, and darkness picked her up and whirled her about like a dancer in a crazy reel. The lean man stepped forward quickly to catch her as she fell.

Footloose after drawing his wages from the Circle T in late fall, Dave Garrison had wandered northeast, for no better reason than that he didn't have to buck the north winds directly all the way to Kansas. He had it in his mind to look up Bix Jordan at his place up on the Big Wichita. Jordan might need a winter hand, or know of someone who did. The first storm holed Garrison up at Big Spring for a week, and the second caught him in the open plains south of the Brazos.

It was only then, losing his way temporarily in the storm, that he realized he had been shunted onto familiar terrain. He came to the Brazos and followed its south bank. Too many years had passed, and blood left no permanent mark in the sand. He believed that he was close to the bend in the river where the little wagon train had been ambushed, but even the skeletons of the burned wagons had vanished, the remaining wood plundered for someone's fire, the enduring metal of harness or wheel rims claimed for another purpose or buried by shifting sands or the fresh fall of snow. Garrison rode past the site without recognition. Only when he came to a line of cedar brakes at the base of a conical bluff did he know for sure where he was. He had climbed that promontory to reconnoiter and from there he had witnessed the massacre.

Looking back, he tried to recollect exactly where it had happened. He had no trouble remembering the girl.

That had been a time of Indian troubles, with Kiowas and Comanches hitting the wagons all summer along the Fort Smith-to-Albuquerque road and its offshoots, the more southerly emigrant wagon trails. Garrison, riding alone, had been aware of Comanche sign for two days, and he had wondered what they were tracking. He rode carefully, keeping below any ridge line or high place, his eyes watchful. When he came upon the freshly cut trail of the wagons, he knew what the Indians were up to, and that the wagons were in trouble. On their swift, tireless ponies the Comanches were literally riding rings around the slower-moving train, like any pack of hunters circling its prey, waiting for the right moment to pull the noose tight.

Following the wagon trail, Garrison found there were only three of them—a small party to be crossing this wilderness during a time of unrest. Six or seven wagons made a handy number in traveling. More than that often meant trouble in foraging for their animals, be they mules or horses or oxen. And that many wagons made up a group bristling with enough guns to discourage anything but a large war party. But three wagons were a tempting prize for an eager war leader.

The wagons had been hit while they were crossing the Brazos. Two had reached the south bank. The third was still in the water, and it spilled over as the driver tried to turn back toward illusory safety. Wagon and horses, people and their possessions floundered in the river. Sacks spilled their stores of powder and grains, sugar and coffee and flour. Trunks filled with clothes and the treasured accumulation of a lifetime broke open, loosing their contents into the stream.

Watching from the bluff far to the east, Garrison was sickened by the spectacle as the Comanches struck quick and hard, pinning down the survivors of the two wagons that had made it to the riverbank. In minutes it was over. He counted at least a dozen warriors in the Comanche party, and there were only a handful of armed pilgrims to answer the attack. The one who had been driving the spilled wagon was shot before he got out of the water. A woman who had been with him was dragged screaming from the river. Two of the other defenders went down in the first furious attack by the Indians. The remaining two men held out for as long as they could, firing from the cover of a fallen wagon. But they could not cover all sides of their perimeter, and a young Indian slipped behind them, using the brow of the riverbank as cover. He shot one of the survivors before the remaining man could answer his fire. Then the other Comanches swarmed over the lone armed white man. He had time only to turn his weapon toward his wife and fire a single shot.

One other woman was dragged from one of the wagons and thrown to the ground beside the one who had been carried from the river. A child was torn from her grasp and brutally slain.

From his distant bluff Dave Garrison watched all this with helpless anger. He was too far away to reach the wagons before they were overwhelmed. He hadn't caught up in time to warn them. Still, he had to fight off the urge to ride screaming at the Comanches, taking as many of them as he could before he went down.

In the end he had stayed where he was. He had fought too many battles of his own not to recognize a foolish and empty gesture for what it was.

The Indians were joyfully plundering the wagons when Garrison saw a flash of white along the riverbank east of the point where the attack had come. At first he thought it was only a dress, spilled from one of the trunks when it tumbled into the river and carried downstream on the current. Then he saw the dress move, burrowing deeper under some protective brush at the edge of the stream.

The Comanches burned the wagons. They spent the rest of the afternoon celebrating their triumph and taking turns with the two surviving women, whose screams became more broken and feeble as the day waned. Garrison was puzzled when the Indians seemed in no hurry to leave. They made camp near the smoking wagons. When he wormed close to that camp after dark, he discovered from the voices and antics of the victors why they had lingered so long. They had found a jug of whiskey in one of the wagons.

He wondered how many of them he could kill, if they were drunk enough.

One of the braves dressed himself in a woman's dress and bonnet, in which he did a victory dance to the raucous delight of his companions. The woman from whom he had taken the dress tried to escape, naked, across the river. He caught her before she had gotten five yards from the riverbank. A knife flashed, dripping silver in the moonlight and then shining dark.

Garrison wondered why the other woman no longer made any sound. When he crawled close enough, he saw her lying crumpled on the ground near one of the gutted wagons, and he knew that she had been an earlier victim.

Grimly he turned back to the river.

He found the girl hiding in the brush about a quarter mile downstream from the Indian camp. When he peered over the bank directly above her, her mouth was already open as if to scream, but no sound emerged even though her throat was working. Garrison reached out quickly, clamped his hand over her mouth, and slid down the bank to her side.

He held her that way for a long time, whispering to her as she first fought him and then went rigid in his grasp.

He told her that she was safe now, that he would let no harm come to her, that she must not make a sound or the Comanches would hear and come searching for them, that their only chance was to remain where they were until the Indians slept.

After a while she seemed to relax, and he was able to take the risk of removing his hand from her mouth. She remained silent. Her eyes, wide and staring, never left his face.

In the darkest hour of the night, when the Comanche camp had been quiet for an hour—the jug long empty, Garrison surmised—he lifted the girl into his arms and set off downstream, keeping to the water near the bank so there would be no suspicious tracks to catch a sharp eye in the morning. The girl was about thirteen or fourteen years old, he judged, with fine features and a slender body and a remarkable spill of golden hair. She was as light as a blanket in his arms, and as soft a burden. She had still not spoken, even when he asked her her name. Garrison had not pursued his questioning, since every whisper in the stillness of the night was a potential danger of discovery.

He stayed in the river until his arms and shoulders ached and his legs were dragging against the pull of the water. At last, perhaps a mile from the site of the massacre, he wearily climbed the bank and set the girl down under the shelter of a lightning-blasted cottonwood. He sat on the bank and sourly emptied the water from his boots. They would dry as hard as boards.

When he looked up, the girl was watching him. The intensity of her gaze made him uncomfortable. Like most cowhands, he was not accustomed to being around women or young girls very much, with the exception of rare forays into a town crib or a cantina near the border.

"You didn't have to carry me all that way," she said. To his relief her voice was level and calm.

He gave a derisive snort. "If that's so, why didn't you say somethin'? Your mouth was open for use the whole way."

"That's not true."

"Way it looked to me."

"I didn't . . . I was scared. What did you expect?"

"So was I."

She stared at him for a long moment in silence before she said, softly, "I don't believe it."

"Well, you oughta believe it. Anyways, children aren't supposed to contradict their elders."

"I'm not a child!" she retorted.

"If you kinda raise that yell of yours just one notch higher, we'll have Comanche company for breakfast."

Even in the darkness he could see her flinch, but the comment had been deliberate. The warning was valid enough. On such a night as this, windless and still, sounds carried over surprising distances across the open plain. But just as importantly, although he was not sure just how to talk to her—the rough humor that passed for conversation among cowhands seemed awkward here—his instinct told him that it was best not to coddle her fear. She seemed to be a lot tougher than her wispy slenderness suggested, for she had come through a shattering horror with her head up and her pride intact. But that might be only a surface thing. Garrison knew that grief and terror were more consuming and terrible when they were buried or hidden. What these Comanches had done was awful enough, but the girl had to live with the memory, one way or another.

He saw the girl staring back across the darkened prairie, and a shiver passed through her body. He said, "Was that your ma they hauled out of the river?"

"Yes."

"She's dead now," Garrison said bluntly. "They can't hurt her anymore. They're all dead, 'cepting you. Nothin' we can do for them now, save come back and bury 'em when it's safe. I know it isn't easy, but you have to think of yourself now. You're alive."

"I . . . I don't know as I want to be . . . anymore."

"You do. Maybe you don't know it yet, but you do."

She began to weep then, almost soundlessly, as if she were instinctively making certain that her sobs would not be heard. Garrison didn't know what to do about it, but after a while he took her into his arms and held her gently until the crying stopped and the shuddering spasms ended.

~ 3 ~

The next day, when the Indians had gone, Garrison came back with the girl and found a shovel in one of the blackened piles of ashes. He buried the dead in a common grave near the river, in a sandy hollow that, in the late afternoon, caught the dappled shade of a cottonwood.

The girl's name, he had learned, was Patricia Lovell, and it was the Lovell wagon that had overturned in the river. It had come to rest on a sandbar, and the girl tried to rescue some of her family's possessions that had not been lost to the river or the Comanches. Gently Garrison had to deny her hopes. The Indians had taken all the animals from the wagons except for one dead mule. He and the girl would have to ride double, and they were days from any settlement. His horse would be burdened enough carrying the two of them. In the end the girl came away with a portrait of her parents in a tin frame and a small bundle of her own clothes. The rest—all that she had possessed and known in her short life—she left behind.

They rode together for six days, traveling slowly, for Garrison remained wary of other Comanche raiders in the area and he did not want to punish his horse. Gradually Patricia Lovell became more at ease with him, and in his turn Garrison grew to like and admire the girl. He respected her resilience and the tart way she stood up for herself when he teased her. After the first few days she was able to talk more freely about herself and her parents, and Garrison heard the familiar story of their struggle to survive on a hard-scrabble dirt farm, the decision to come West, the high hopes that had carried them through the hardships of the long journey. She talked about her father, a lively man whose fiddle she had found smashed in the wagon, and her mother, until Garrison came to feel almost as if he had known them. Then, almost imperceptibly, she began to talk less about herself and to query him about his own past, his adventures, his life as soldier and scout, rainbow chaser and wandering cowhand. He didn't realize what was happening until one night when he awoke suddenly, in some alarm, and found her sitting up by their low campfire, a blanket wrapped around her shoulders, staring at him in a strange way.

The meaning of that stare became clear in the days that followed, in long silences that matched his normal taciturn ways, in laughter too eager over his mild attempts at humor, in the warm press of her body against his as they rode together. He reasoned that she had come to see him as a kind of hero, her rescuer, and that she had attached herself to him in an exaggerated way because of that. The knowledge made him uncomfortable, for he had done nothing to save her parents or the others in the ill-fated wagon train, and she had been saved more by good luck than by any heroics on his part. Still, there was no escaping it: The foolish girl thought she was in love with him.

At that time Dave Garrison was nearly twice her age, and he felt even older, except when, sometimes, he would catch a glimpse of the woman she might become. She was already pretty, and, though slender, she was filling out like a young woman. There were times when, as they rode together, he would find himself becoming too aware of her warmth brushing against him, of their bodies rocking together in the slow rhythm of the horse's gait. He took to walking more, punishing his feet, explaining that old Blackie was tired of carrying two people all the time. Her young-old eyes, sober, seemed to see right through his clumsy explanations.

It had to end, and soon. Yet, when he saw the town at last, mixed with his expected relief there was also a pang of . . . something. He had grown fond of the girl, no denying. There was a gentleness in her that had touched him deeply. He woke early, and he had found an anticipation of that moment when she would open her eyes slowly to the morning light and wrinkle her nose at the smell of the coffee he had ready. At night, by their campfire, he had discovered a quiet pleasure in the play of light over her face and neck.

It was just that she was so young, and had mistaken gratitude for something else. And he was a wanderer. She would forget him soon enough, he was sure. In the meantime, it was right that she should have a proper upbringing, proper schooling, proper shelter.

She had no family, he had learned, other than her parents. There was a distant cousin or so, but she seemed not to know how they could be reached and had no interest in finding them. She seemed quite placidly to accept the fact that Garrison was now responsible for her. In the manner of the very young, she did not look beyond the next sunrise, except to dream. She saw no trouble ahead.

Garrison found the answer to his problem at the Bauers' rooming house, where he took Patricia Lovell to find her a soft bed and a good hot meal that first night in Cedar Point. It seemed a peaceful little town, more dust than progress, with a stage stop, a brick-front bank, a small schoolhouse, the usual supply stores, a blacksmith's shop, a tannery, a gunsmith's, two churches and four saloons. Garrison brushed aside the passing thought that he would have as soon settled down in a dust bowl as live in Cedar Point himself. It was different, he reasoned, for a girl. No young woman could stand the rough, uncertain and haphazard life he enjoyed. Town was the place for her.

And Emma Bauer was a friendly woman, plump and white as bread dough, with a cheerful warmth that explained the popularity of her place. That and the plain, hearty fare that made her dining table groan. Henry Bauer didn't seem of much account. He had busy eyes and a mouth that smiled at the wrong times, but he jumped when Emma spoke his name. (She called him "Mr. Bauer" every time Garrison heard her speak to him or about him.) Garrison thought the woman had a good heart, and she might be able to advise him what to do about the girl.

After the Lovell girl slept that night, luxuriating in a feather bed after weeks in a wagon and recent nights rolling up in a blanket on the ground, Garrison talked to Emma Bauer. As his hunch had suggested, she was a warmly sympathetic woman. She was also approaching forty years old and childless. Before their talk was over, she had eagerly agreed to take the girl in herself. Patricia would have a good home there, Garrison need never fear.

Garrison then did one thing that he would later ques-

tion and regret for a long time. He had said nothing to
Patricia Lovell about his plans. She had gone to bed
promising to be up early to curry Blackie and see that
every last burr was out of his tail. Garrison, grinning, had
said that Blackie would enjoy that, since he seldom got
much of what you might call grooming. Long before
dawn Garrison saddled the horse, burrs and all, and rode
out. He carried with him a sense of guilt, a knowledge
that he did not want to face telling the girl that he was
going on alone.

There was nothing else he could do, he told himself.
She would forget him soon enough.

4

Eight years later, the first blow of the new storm chased
Dave Garrison into Cedar Point. Except that it was winter
instead of summer, with snow blowing around instead
of dust, the little town didn't seem to have changed
very much. The same stores and saloons were still doing
business. One of the churches was boarded up, but the
other survived. The Bauers' rooming house was still where
he remembered it.

Garrison did not go there directly. Without trying to
explain his reasons to himself, he felt the need for a bath
and a shave and a change of clothes. He asked Tom
Secomb, the barber, if he knew the Lovell girl who had
lived with the Bauers. Secomb said he was new in town,
there less than a year. He knew of the girl—right pretty,
as he remembered—but he couldn't say where she was or
how she was getting on. Garrison wondered why the man
was being evasive.

A clean shirt, a bath and a shave could make the
weariest rider feel like a new man, and Garrison walked

over to the boardinghouse with a feeling of anticipation, an eagerness unexpected after so many years. She would be a young woman now. He was curious to know how she had fared. Even the weather seemed to accommodate his mood, for the snow had stopped and the sky had lifted. The town lay crisp and clean and quiet under its white blanket.

He was late for the noon meal, but he was in hopes that Emma Bauer would rustle up some leftovers when she remembered him.

He had his first disturbing intuition when he reached the house. Houses, like people, could age and weather gracefully or poorly. This one showed neglect on close examination, in the broken step of the porch, in clapboard sides badly in need of paint, in a window boarded up instead of being repaired.

Henry Bauer, looking grayer but otherwise much the same, opened the door. There was a surliness in his manner that Garrison did not remember. He stared at Garrison without pretense at welcome. "You're too late for dinner," he said, and started to close the door.

Garrison stopped it with his boot. "I'd like to see Mrs. Bauer," he said.

A sharp but nameless suspicion quickened in Bauer's eyes. "What for?"

"I reckon you don't remember me," Garrison said. "Name of Garrison. I left a girl with you and Mrs. Bauer a long spell back. Seven, eight years ago, it was. She was—"

"I remember you now." Bauer appraised him critically, as if he were searching for something he couldn't find. "Hell, I wouldn't have recognized you. The way that girl used to moon over you, I'd have expected you to be at least a foot taller and wider, and a sight more . . ." The list of expectations trailed off. "It's the first Mrs. Bauer you'd be looking for. She passed on five years ago."

The news jolted Garrison. Such a simple, everyday possibility had not occurred to him. "I'm sorry, I didn't know."

"No reason you should. And if it's the girl you're after, you won't find her here neither."

Garrison frowned. "Can you tell me where she is now?"

"Henry? Who are you talkin' to out there?" The voice was querulous, edgy. The door was suddenly flung open by a hand reaching past Henry Bauer's shoulder, and a thin-bodied woman with a very full bust appeared behind him. "What does he want?" she demanded, staring at Garrison but not addressing him.

"He's looking for Trish." Henry Bauer's snappish reply suggested that the two carried on a running warfare.

"That tramp? What does he want with her? As if I couldn't figure that out," she added with a contemptuous sniff.

Dave Garrison did not particularly like Henry Bauer, but for an instant he felt something almost like pity for the man. The woman beside him must be the new Mrs. Bauer, and the petulant unhappiness in her face was in sharp contrast with what Garrison remembered of Emma Bauer. This woman, younger, had china-doll features and must once have been pretty—perhaps had been only a few years ago, when Henry Bauer presumably married her. Her prettiness was warped by her dissatisfaction with life, which revealed itself in her eyes and their shadows and in the sullen pull of her thin-lipped mouth. Emma Bauer had been a warm, abundant woman; this one would offer little warmth or comfort for a cold night, Garrison thought. And little peace during the day.

"Maybe you can tell me where I'd find her," he suggested mildly.

"We don't have to tell him anything," the woman said. "She's nothin' to do with us anymore—and good riddance, too."

"Now, Irene, there's no harm in telling him—"

"Then tell him the truth! Tell him when she couldn't have you she was ready to wriggle up to anythin' with pants on." For the first time Irene Bauer then spoke directly to Garrison. "She got to thinkin' she was too good to put in an honest day's work in this house, if you want to know. I guess it was a sight easier liftin' her skirts over to the Silver Palace."

"Is that where I'd find her now?" Garrison asked coolly.

"She doesn't live in town anymore," Henry Bauer interjected, as if to head off another caustic comment from his wife. "She's . . . married."

"Married!" Irene Bauer sniffed. "That's puttin' a nice wrapping around it, but it don't change what's inside. She's no more married to that Virgil Pryor than any other saloon hussy. She was askin' for trouble, and that's what she found. She won't hear any talk of a preacher from him. He likes his good times too much. When he's through with her, likely she'll come whinin' back here, lookin' to be taken in again."

"When that happens," Garrison drawled, "I'm sure she'll get what's comin' to her."

Irene Bauer looked at him sharply, as if she were not sure whether or not to take affront. Then she said, "You're lettin' in the cold, Henry." And she reached past him to close the door in Garrison's face.

~~~ 5 ~~~

The bright expectation had left Dave Garrison when he retraced his steps from the boardinghouse toward the center of town. He had always thought fondly of Emma Bauer's place, believing that Patricia Lovell must surely have found warmth and love there. The discovery that that period of happiness had been short-lived sobered and saddened him.

He followed the recent rut made by a wagon in the fresh layer of snow along the main street until he hopped onto the boardwalk. Without deliberate intent he soon found himself in front of the Silver Palace. After a brief hesitation he stepped inside.

On this cold day the place had a cheerless atmosphere. A steady draft whistled through a wide crack under the storm door. There were only a few men present. Two women, neither of them very young, were idly playing cards at a table in one corner, huddled inside heavy coats.

Two men at a table near the bar looked at Garrison with open curiosity. Both were town men, by the look of their clothes, settled in as if they had no better place to be on a winter's day. They were idle and bored, eager to break the tedium of the time with fresh talk, and it required only a brief nod from Garrison for him to receive an invitation to join them at their table. He called for a bottle, warmed his belly with the first drink, and left the bottle on the table.

The conversation was easy, running to that morning's fall of "Oklahoma rain" and the general unpredictability of Texas weather. Garrison waited patiently before he brought the talk around to Patricia Lovell, who had lived with the Bauers and later worked at the Palace.

The town men exchanged quick glances. "Trish Lovell? You know her?" Raymond Soule asked.

"That's right."

"Funny thing, I don't seem to recollect seein' you before. You hear that, Tom?"

Tom McGrath nodded to indicate that he had heard. Something of his indolent manner had left him. "It sure is a small world," he commented. "You just passin' through our town, Mr. Garrison?"

Garrison nodded. "I thought I'd look up the girl, see how things have turned out for her." He paused. "I hear she's livin' with a man name of Pryor."

"Well, now," Soule said slowly, "what would that be to you, Mr. Garrison, if you don't mind my askin'?"

"Just curious, I reckon."

"I wouldn't be too curious where Virgil Pryor is concerned, if I was you. Just friendly advice, is all."

Garrison wondered about the caution that seemed to have overcome the two town men. He was reminded of the same reticence in the barber when he had inquired about Patricia Lovell.

In the momentary silence the outer door opened, letting in a gust of cold air and a small, grizzled cowhand, hunched over as if in pain. The door blew shut and the little man hobbled past the bar and Garrison's table, moving on one bowed, gimpy leg and crutches. His other leg was encased and held rigid in a board splint. The silence held, making the drag of foot and scrape of crutch the center of attention until the crippled man had reached a table at the back of the saloon. He signaled for a drink, and the bartender carried a bottle over to his table. The bartender poured one drink into a glass and took the bottle away with him, suggesting that the old-timer's credit might be as limited as coin in his pockets.

"Seems like a lot of people have taken an interest in Virgil lately," Raymond Soule said. "There was three others passin' through. Day before yesterday, wasn't it, Tom?"

"Day before yesterday," McGrath agreed.

"Is that so?" Garrison did not indicate any particular interest in the news. "It was the girl I asked about, not Pryor."

"That's so, but the way things are, you might just as well ask about the one as the other. Seein' as how Trish has been, well, livin' with Pryor, like you said."

"Is the Pryor place nearby?" Garrison asked.

"Not so far," Soule answered after a moment. "But you won't likely find him there. Ain't nobody seen him in . . . must be since the fall roundup, isn't that about it, Tom? Two months, I'd guess."

"Two months, easy," Tom McGrath said.

Garrison smiled. "Did those other strangers was askin' around about Pryor learn as much as I am?"

Soule glanced at him quickly, trying to read his expression. A cautious smile touched his lips, and he put his hand to his face as if to cover the reaction. "Well, now, there wasn't much anyone could tell 'em, seein' as how Virg Pryor's not been seen in these parts lately."

"He seems to have a lot of friends."

"Well, I guess you could say Virgil grew up hereabouts. Everybody knows him."

"He takes good care of Patricia? Treats her right?"

There was another silence. Soule glanced at the bottle on the table, and Garrison said, "Will you have another drink on me, long as the bottle's handy?"

"Maybe I'll do that," Soule said, but he did not reach for the bottle in spite of his longing glance. "You haven't said why it was you wanted to hear about Trish."

"I was the one brought her here," Garrison said. "Eight years ago, that was, after her folks were killed by Comanches."

Raymond Soule's jaw dropped. "You're the one? Well, why didn't you say so? You hear, Tom?"

"If that don't beat all," McGrath said, voicing the same surprise.

"Maybe I'll have that drink after all," Soule said, with something like relief in his tone. The atmosphere was suddenly more relaxed. "Isn't that something," he said as he poured a drink for himself and his friend before he pushed the bottle back toward Garrison. "So you're the one rescued that girl from the Injuns. A lucky thing you happened along when you did, Mr. Garrison. That was a hard time for a young girl, and that's a fact."

"I reckon maybe it was almost as sorry a day when Emma Bauer passed on," Garrison said, testing the ground further.

The town men exchanged another glance, and Raymond Soule grinned. "You get one of the new Mrs. Bauer's tongue-lashings, did you? Well, I'll tell you somethin', Mr. Garrison, you're not the first. And you're right, it was a sorry day for that girl when Emma took sick." He paused, his chuckle fading. "It was a sorry day for Henry, too."

"For anyone likes a good meal under his belt," McGrath rumbled reminiscently. "Emma Bauer sure knew how to burn a biscuit."

"You want to know about Trish Lovell, Mr. Garrison," Soule said, reverting to his earlier volubility. "A nice, pretty girl, that one. Worked here at the Palace for a spell after Irene Bauer kicked her out. Irene, she had that girl doin' the town's laundry, workin' her down to a stick, until she saw the way Trish was growin' into a pretty thing. Irene wouldn't trust Henry around any other woman. She tried every way to make the girl leave, and finally she just trumped up a quarrel and forced her out."

"Henry Bauer didn't object?"

"Oh, Henry shouts at her. He'd never have raised his voice to Emma, but them two carry on now like a couple of squirrels. But all he's doin' is making noise. Henry never did have a pinch of sand in him."

"I see." Garrison watched Soule pour himself and McGrath another drink without invitation. "So that's how she come to take up with this man Pryor—the one who has so many friends."

Raymond Soule glanced nervously around the room, although nothing had changed and there seemed little reason for his nervousness. It seemed to come over him, Garrison thought, whenever Virgil Pryor's name was mentioned.

"It ain't that Virgil has so many friends exactly, Mr. Garrison. But that girl does. A sweet girl, she is." Soule hesitated, looked at McGrath for help that didn't come, and shook himself, as if he were anxiously shedding an unwanted burden. "You're in luck, Mr. Garrison. You want to know about Trish Lovell and Virgil Pryor, there's one man can tell you better than any other. He's sittin' right over there, the one at the back table with the broken leg. You tell him just what you told us, so he'll know it's all right. That's Pegleg Parks, and he thinks as much of that girl as any of us."

Garrison stared in surprise at the crippled man in the back of the room. Parks was brooding over his empty glass, unaware of the attention. Thoughtfully Garrison said, "Did you happen to mention Parks to those other strangers?"

Raymond Soule drew himself up stiffly, his thick muttonchops quivering indignantly. "No sirree, Mr. Garrison. Not them. They had a smell about 'em, and that's a fact. The smell of trouble."

"Same as Virgil," McGrath said unexpectedly.

Soule looked at him somewhat aghast. He glanced furtively over his shoulder at some invisible danger, then nodded jerkily. "They didn't learn a thing," he said, "exceptin' that there was no reason to hang around, seein' as Virgil hasn't been seen in these parts for two months or more. Fact is, Mr. Garrison, there isn't one of us would like to see any more trouble come to Trish Lovell than she already has."

"What trouble might that be?" Garrison prodded gently.

But Soule looked away vaguely. Neither he nor McGrath would answer the question, or meet Garrison's eye. He wondered what kind of man the girl had chosen, who could inspire so much fear in his absence. After a moment of speculation, Garrison picked up his bottle and carried it to the table in the back of the room.

6

An hour later Dave Garrison was riding out of Cedar Point, heading south. The sky was high and bright when he left, with no snow falling, and the landscape was a harsh brilliance of endless white, hard against his eyes. He asked himself what he thought he was doing. It was no business of his anymore, what happened to Patricia Lovell. His involvement with her had been accidental, a chancy thing, long ago.

Still, he had never forgotten those days together, after the girl had begun to emerge from the shock of her parents' death. Pleasant days. He remembered Patricia Lovell as pretty and brave and sunny-natured. He remembered her as being on the very edge of womanhood . . . too near, perhaps, to be riding alone with a man. He had always hoped that things had gone well with her.

Pegleg Parks had quickly dispelled that comfortable illusion. Cautious at first, he had loosened up as soon as Garrison told him who he was and then poured a drink into the old man's empty glass.

"So you're Garrison. Trish would sure be happy to see

you, I reckon. She used to talk about you, as I remember."

"She did?" Garrison felt foolishly pleased.

"That's a fact. I remember once, she'd washed out her hair and it was a sight to behold, like it was pure gold. Pryor said somethin' to her, and she laughed and said if it wasn't for you, she'd have lost it all to the Comanches." Parks paused abruptly. "I don't reckon she ever said that again."

"Why is that?"

Parks' eyes became vague. "He didn't like it."

Garrison frowned, disturbed as much by the things people left unsaid about Virgil Pryor as by the words actually spoken. He said, "Folks hereabouts seem to worry a lot about rilin' Mr. Pryor."

The gimpy old-timer nodded. "You go walkin' through a nest of rattlesnakes, you wouldn't go out of your way to step on the meanest of 'em whilst he was sleepin', I reckon." He paused. "I'm not speakin' against Pryor. I work for him, and that's that. But he's not one you'd like to rile, Mr. Garrison. You mind if'n I have another drink of your whiskey?"

"Help yourself."

"Talkin' makes a man dry." Parks filled his glass until the whiskey sloshed over the rim. He bent down to sip a little so as not to spill any before picking up the glass. "Was you thinkin' of tryin' to see Mrs. Pryor?"

"I'd thought of it."

"You'd be a damned fool to let Pryor ever catch you there with her," Parks said.

"But she's alone?"

Parks shifted uncomfortably in his chair. "Far as I know. I don't like it any better'n you do. A woman shouldn't be alone like that, this kind of weather. That damned fool Ramon lit a shuck 'fore I ever got hurt. That Mex is the only other hand Pryor kept around for the winter," the old man explained. "He's got family down near the border, goes to see 'em every once in a while. No tellin' when he'll be back."

"And Pryor's been gone a couple months?"

"Least that long," Parks said vaguely. "He does that. He'll come back when he's ready." The little man's pale, watery eyes studied Garrison. "He'd better find Trish there, if she knows what's good for her. And he'd better not find you, or any other man."

If the snow had still been falling, it was doubtful that Garrison would have set out for the Pryor place the way he did. It made too little sense, and there were too many arguments against the impulse that pushed him. He was disturbed by some of the things he had heard, the hint of sympathy in their voices when anyone spoke about the young woman in connection with Virgil Pryor. But it was no business of his. She was no longer a girl alone; she was a woman now. There had been a deceptive lull in the storm, however. The sky had lifted and brightened, the wind had slackened. And Dave Garrison had always been a man who followed his impulses—a drifter, some might have said, with no more direction than summer dust or winter snow blowing on the wind. He wormed directions out of Pegleg Parks and decided he could make it to the Pryor place well before dark. He would just make sure the young woman was all right. He'd say hello, and then he would move along. He would rest easier, somehow, if he had seen her.

He was more than halfway there, by his reckoning, when the wind quickened and turned colder with the stunning suddenness of a norther. Dark, heavy clouds moved in swiftly. It began to snow again, and before long Garrison knew that he was in some difficulty.

He thought again of turning back, but he was a stubborn man once he had set his mind one way, a fact that went contrary to the common notion of a drifter. Besides, he told himself, hat pulled down, head bent and collar up against the whirling snow and the bitter wind, the Pryor outfit had to be closer now than town. If he didn't want to end up a frozen statue, he had best keep moving the way he was.

Sometimes, even when you had made a choice that started to look foolhardy, there was no turning back.

CHAPTER 2

The soddy was tucked into the shelter of a steep rise, which formed the back wall and part of two sides of the structure. The protruding portion of each side wall and the front of the house had been built of mud bricks. The poles of the ceiling supported a sod roof that was certainly snug enough but would, Garrison surmised, seep or drip during any prolonged spring thaw or summer rain. There was one glass window in the front wall to the left of the door. The place must have been built a while back, during a period of more prevalent Indian troubles. There were firing ports on three sides. Their slide covers, long unused, had been plastered with mud around the edges to seal out drafts.

The inside was essentially one big room, dominated by the fireplace, which filled one end. It also served for cooking. A horse blanket hung from a rope stretched across the opposite end of the room, providing a rudimentary screen for a sleeping alcove. The blanket had already been drawn aside, and Garrison stepped past it to lay the young woman gently onto the single bed built into the alcove.

She stirred almost immediately, and her eyelids fluttered open. She stared up at Garrison, her blue eyes momentarily wide and blank. Then comprehension flooded them.

"I don't know what came over me," Trish Lovell said, sitting up abruptly, flustered, pushing the heavy fall of golden hair away from her face. She had grown up even prettier than her youthful promise, Garrison thought.

"I reckon you thought you was seein' a ghost."

She rose quickly. Garrison stepped back to make room, brushing against the suspended horse blanket. There was a strange awkwardness between them, and something more, a man-and-woman awareness so sudden and strong that it left Garrison confused. He felt the stunned surprise of a rider unexpectedly thrown, wondering how he had been so abruptly parted from the saddle leather.

Trish Lovell moved past him into the room. Her cheeks were pink, and her blue-eyed gaze now avoided his. As she got over the lingering astonishment of waking up on her bed with Garrison looming over her in perplexed concern, a stiffness became more obvious in her manner. "I suppose that was it, me being alone here, and you blowing in out of the snow."

"I heard you was alone. It's why I come by. I wanted to . . ." The explanation drew up lame. Garrison was still not very sure why he had come. "I wanted to see you—see how you were."

"I can see why you'd rush through a storm to find me," she commented dryly. "Let's see now, how long has it been?"

"Seven, eight years, I reckon," Garrison murmured, hearing the biting edge in her question.

"Eight."

"Well . . . it's been a while," he admitted. He felt obscurely guilty, a feeling that went all the way back to that early morning when he had sneaked out of Cedar Point without telling a young girl that he was leaving. But surely she had understood that necessity long ago, he told himself, a conviction weakened by her lack of friendliness. "I just never got to come back this way, seems like."

"The wind didn't blow this way," she said for him.

Garrison smiled. "I reckon that's about it. That don't mean I forgot. I always wondered how you'd got on, and that's a fact."

"I've done fine," she said tartly. "Just fine."

The words were cold, denying the self-consciousness of a moment ago, denying any remembered warmth between them, denying the substance of Garrison's concern and his reason for being there.

She crossed toward the fireplace, a slim young woman who was, Garrison realized ruefully, a complete stranger to him, as he was to her. She busied herself over the fire, brushing ashes from the wood coals and bringing a heavy iron skillet on tricorner legs closer to the fire. There were no words of welcome, no sign of pleasure at seeing him again after so long. Garrison shrugged off his tug of disappointment. What did he expect? She was right. Eight years was a long time. She had been a child eight years ago.

Still, the disappointment lingered.

"Well, you've come a long way and I expect you're hungry. Not that I have much to offer you."

"I ate in town," Garrison said. "I'm not hungry. Never meant to trouble you," he added by way of apology. "I won't be stayin' long."

She swung the kettle on its arm, placing it over the fire, before she turned to face him. The heat from the coals had deepened the flush in her face. "Don't be foolish. You can't go out in that storm. And you've ridden far enough to empty the trough again. It's not like you ate at Emma Bauer's table."

For the first time, as she mentioned Emma Bauer's name, her cold manner seemed to relent a little. There might even have been a trace of mocking amusement in her eyes for an instant, and Garrison smiled back at it. "I was late for the noon meal at the old Bauer place. Had to settle for a tongue-lashing, and eats at the cafe. From what I hear, I didn't miss much." He paused a moment before adding, "I was sorry to hear about Mrs. Bauer."

"How could you be? You didn't even know . . ." She broke off the sharp reply. "Maybe you are sorry, I don't know. I've no call to snap at you, I reckon."

Hearing the bitterness in her saddened Garrison. The girl he had rescued eight years ago seemed almost lost in this young woman. Even after witnessing the deaths of her parents, that girl had been surprisingly resilient, defiant, ready to spit in life's eye if need be. What had wrought so drastic a change? The crushing loneliness of this prairie could do that to a woman in time, but Patricia Lovell was too young still to have been defeated so soon. The trouble with the Bauers, then? Or did it have more to do with Virgil Pryor?

"It went bad for you after she passed on, I guess."

"It's no concern of yours, Mr. Garrison." She used his name for the first time, and he felt a slight surprise that she remembered it. "Anyway, that was a long time ago. It's water under the bridge, isn't it? I never went hungry, and I had some schooling and religion and a roof over my head. That's what you figured on, I reckon." She paused, her gaze candid and challenging. "Or did you just run off because you didn't want to be saddled with any more trouble?"

"It seemed like the best thing for you," Garrison murmured.

"For me?" She gave an abrupt laugh. "I suppose it did. Stop looking so hangdog, Mr. Garrison. You've nothing to blame yourself for. You couldn't have known how it would work out. Anyway, I'm . . . married now, and I'm

bein' taken care of just fine. And I *am* glad to see you,
even if I haven't acted very hospitable. I guess I'm just
not used to receiving company out here. Not many come
this way. Take off your coat, Mr. Garrison, before you
melt away. I won't see you go hungry into that storm,
and you might as well figure on being here for a spell before it breaks."

He hesitated, reluctant to leave but yet not comfortable about staying. Then the wind outside picked something up and blew it against the front wall of the soddy.
There was a heavy thump. Garrison saw Trish Lovell give
a start, something like panic fleetingly in her eyes.

He shrugged out of his heavy coat, hung it on a
wooden peg beside the door, and brushed away the melt-
ing snow that trickled down his neck. Maybe it was none
of his business anymore, as she herself had said, but he
knew that she had revealed little of the truth about her
current situation. There was more to her isolation and
fear than she let on.

He would stay for supper anyway. And after that? The
wind had blown him here, and gusted up to cause him to
stay. He would see which way it blew when his belly was
full.

2

They talked little during the meal. Trish Lovell brought
out some side meat and cut generous portions, which she
laid in the deep iron skillet. When she had finished, the
slab of meat that was left seemed pitifully small. Garrison
wondered if there was any more where that had come
from. Yet something told him that he should not protest.
Now that it was decided he would stay a while, Trish
Lovell seemed determined to prove to him that she was

doing just fine, as she had claimed. Once she made light of his having come so far out of his way for so little in return, and Garrison sensed the pride that compelled her to put the best possible face on her situation.

But even that fact disturbed him. What kind of man would leave a woman alone on this frontier for months on end, especially in winter? Who was this man she chose to call her husband?

The aromas of side pork and potatoes and onions mingling in the skillet quickly filled the small house and started rumblings in Garrison's stomach. By the time they sat down to eat he was ravenous, and the food was as good as its promise.

So was the coffee. Garrison's first tentative sip—he had been recalling a young girl's disastrous attempts to make camp coffee eight years ago—turned into eager swallows.

He reminded her of a morning he had used her undrinkable coffee to douse the campfire. After that he had made coffee himself. "You must've learned how to cook from Emma Bauer."

"She was a fine woman. I learned a lot from her."

"You learned your lessons well when it came to cookin', that's for sure. And brewin' coffee."

"There's carrot cake to go with the coffee."

Garrison saw how pleased she was by the eager way he had wolfed down his meal, and by his compliments. Watching her as she cleared away the dishes from the table after they had eaten, it seemed to him that she was becoming more relaxed with him. Removing that protective stiffness, however, had revealed cares and emotions that had been hidden. Sadness, he thought. Or loneliness.

The storm continued unabated through the evening. It had the effect of isolating the two people in the soddy even more than would normally have been the case. When the wind finally died there was total silence outside, everything muffled by the fall of snow. Garrison began to be uncomfortably aware of their isolation. It was as if this small room with its wood fire had become the center of the universe; for a time nothing else existed. It was impossible not to become more and more conscious of the pretty young woman who sought ineffectually to find ways to keep busy, trying not to be compelled to sit and stare at him. Images of a thin, frightened, desperate girl kept overlapping his glimpses of this grown-up, tight-lipped woman. No sullen pull at her mouth, he thought; she was too proud for that. But a pinched bitterness was visible, and defeat was not too far away.

At length he risked the question paramount in his mind. "What kind of man is he, this Virgil Pryor?"

"I married him, Mr. Garrison."

"That's no answer."

"I don't have to answer."

"No, you don't. Not if you don't want to."

For a moment she hesitated. Then she sank onto one of the two wooden benches facing the table at which they had shared their meal. She began to talk, as if all she had needed was his assurance that she did not have to say anything unless she chose to. "He used to come into the Bauers' place sometimes for his meals when he was in town. I never thought he took notice of me much. He's a handsome man, Virgil is, and you could tell he could just pick and choose. Not that there's so many women in these parts for a man to pick and choose from, but . . . you know Virgil would always just have to grin and wink his eye and he'd find whatever was there."

Her sidelong glance sought Garrison's reaction to this description, but he said nothing. He wondered if he wanted to hear more of the story now, but there was no way to take back his question.

"I got to know him better when I was workin' at the Silver Palace," Trish Lovell went on. "I don't know what you heard in town, Mr. Garrison, but I wasn't doin' . . . anything wrong, if that's what's in your mind. I wasn't any upstairs woman. I was only there to pretty up the place, that's what Tom Hogan said—Tom owns the Palace. Anyways, that's where I was when Virgil begun to pay attention to me. I reckon I grew up while he wasn't lookin', and then he come in one time and saw me, and that's when it started. He'd make a fuss over me whenever he come into the Palace, and . . ." She paused, brushing an imaginary speck of dust from the tabletop, then catching a sheaf of golden hair in the crook of her hand, between thumb and forefinger, and combing it back from her forehead. "He's a lively man, Mr. Garrison. I reckon I never met anybody like him. Oh, there was some folks talked against him, because he grew up hereabouts and he was always kind of wild, but he's not . . . I never believed some of the things said against him." As she went on, it seemed to Garrison that she skirted some areas gingerly, choosing her ground. Virgil Pryor was the kind of man who made everyone step around him carefully, one way or another. "He took me dancin' one summer over to Wheaton, and to the county fair at Fort Worth. He showed me a real good time, Mr. Garrison. I don't know if you can understand that. I never went anywhere, not in all those years since you left me at the Bauers' place. Virgil Pryor took me places and we had good times. He told me I didn't belong at the Palace, that I was too pretty for such a place, and . . ." She broke off, color staining her cheeks. Her glance skidded away from Garrison. "That's how come it was I married him. In the fall it was, a year ago, before he had to go north on business. And he brought me here." She paused, looking around the room as if she were inspecting her house through the eyes of a stranger. "It may not look like much, but it's the first home I ever had of my own."

Garrison said nothing. He felt like a fool for having fancied that she was in some sort of trouble. Virgil Pryor might not be wearing saintly robes, but how many men could, without discomfort?

"I know what you're thinkin', Mr. Garrison," Trish Lovell said. "That it wasn't right for me to be left here alone. But Virgil never meant it to be that way. If it wasn't for Pegleg Parks havin' his accident, and Ramon takin' off like he did at just the wrong time . . ." She was suddenly pensive. "Virgil won't like that. When he finds out . . ."

The unfinished thought hung in the silence. Trish Lovell hugged her body tightly, arms crossed over her chest, as if she felt a sudden chill. She stared at the fire.

Garrison wondered how much of what she had said was truth, and how much was made up of the lies that people constructed to deceive themselves, trying to reconcile what they had with what they wanted, what life finally offered with the dreams they had dreamed. He wondered if she even knew herself. Most people lied to themselves a little, and after a while it was often hard to tell where truth ended and a lie began.

Garrison tried to fool himself less than most people did. Perhaps that was because he asked little of life and therefore could not be disappointed much. He took what came, drawing pleasure from simple things. There was a continuing joy in such familiar, ordinary things as the day's first fire and the aroma of coffee drifting in the fresh morning air. And there was a different joy in the newness of other things. Every morning was new to him. Every hill and canyon and winding trail had its promise and mystery. The land was always changing, always different, the land and the sky and the weather, and there were

places in his wanderings where he could come close to
believing that no man had ever made tracks there before
him.

But was that all he ever wanted? Drifting on had always satisfied him, and he had been content to travel
light. But was that really all? Or had he tricked himself
into believing that was all he wanted, because that was
what he had?

He stared at the young woman's profile limned by the
firelight, at the massive spill of golden hair framing lean,
fine bones of nose and cheek. The tight lips were softer
now, more vulnerable, and there was beauty in the elo-
quent line of her neck, so slender and soft.

He should never have come, he thought. And Trish
Lovell seemed to pluck the words right out of his head.

"You shouldn't have come here, Mr. Garrison."

He was momentarily too startled to answer.

"You can stay the night, but then you'll have to leave.
It wouldn't do if . . . if Virgil found you here. He can be
a . . . a jealous man."

"You ought to move into town. You shouldn't stay the
winter here alone."

"No. He'll be back soon."

"How can you know that?"

"I can feel it. I know." When she looked at him he saw
the troubled conviction in her eyes. "I thought that was
him on the ridge, instead of you."

Garrison frowned, puzzled.

"I saw you earlier on, before you came knocking, up on
that bluff above the canyon. Thought maybe it was a
wolf, or just a ghost, until you came and I heard you
holler out."

Garrison did not reply. In the silence his thoughts returned to Virgil Pryor, and he felt a slow birth of anger.

The girl deserved better than she had chosen. Still, she had made her bed. What else could he do but ride on?

"I'll sleep in the shed," he said at last.

"You'll do nothing of the kind. You'd freeze to death. There's a fire here, and you won't disturb me." She smiled faintly, a little sadly. "It won't be the first time we slept close together, Mr. Garrison."

Later, when he had made a place for himself in a corner of the main room for the night, lying in darkness made liquid by the glow from the banked fire, he stared at the blanket drawn across the far end of the room and the sleeping alcove, and Trish Lovell's last words came back to him. He stirred, restless.

But the last thing he remembered before sleep was what she had said about seeing something—or someone— on the ridge.

He wondered what she had seen. Garrison's approach to the ranch had brought him in from the east, and he had never climbed to the rim above the canyon.

 3

When Garrison woke in Trish Lovell's soddy at first light, while the young woman still slept behind her blanket curtain, he rose quietly, went stiffly to the window and peered out. The snow had stopped before he took to his blankets, and evidently there had been no further fall during the night. The land was a white silence everywhere, as far as the eye could see, all of its shapes mounded and softened. The snow was powder light, lifted easily by any breeze, and it was already drifting into new forms of landscape, piling in softly sculptured buttresses against anything vertical, wall or bluff, post or embankment.

Garrison studied the pure expanse thoughtfully. He worked his hands gently, trying to ease the morning stiffness. The snow bore no tracks of any kind, at least none that he could see from this vantage. There was nothing whatsoever to make a man uneasy or suspicious.

Why then did he have this prickly sensation?

Dave Garrison was a careful man by deeply ingrained habit, not one to dismiss any warning instinct, however unfounded it seemed. He regarded any other course as foolhardy. Of all the animals in the West only one, the grizzly, was disdainful of all others. Because of that arrogance the great bears had been thinned out mercilessly, first by mountain men and then by other hunters. The survivors of the breed had belatedly learned caution, if not fear.

Once, on a scouting mission for the 5th Cavalry in Crook's Arizona campaign, Garrison had been forced to travel alone through hostile Apache country. He rode only at dusk and in the early morning, when it was light enough to see his trail but too dark for him to see—or be seen—for any great distance. In the middle hours of the night, and all through the white heat of the day, he holed up.

On his second night out he came in the last fading twilight to the spring he had been searching for, at the base of some sandstone bluffs. Preparing to make camp, he started to hobble his mare where she could enjoy the patch of grass near the spring. Caution changed his mind and he turned her loose. She wouldn't leave the grass and water. He would be safer elsewhere.

Garrison carried his saddle and gear a short distance until he found a niche in the rocks high above the trail. Then he went back to the spring and, dragging a broken branch behind him, obliterated the scant sign he had left on the hard ground. He climbed up to his hard but hidden bed and slept.

The Apaches came in the middle of the night, silent as ghosts. Garrison, whose sleep was very light, heard only the whisper of a moccasin on the trail just beneath his perch. He woke instantly to an iron-willed stillness. He did not move. He made his breathing shallow, through his open mouth, making no sound.

There were three of them. They found the mare beside the spring but there was no sign of her rider. Hobbles would have been a dead giveaway, but the horse was free and there were no fresh tracks but hers in the dust or on the grass. Even the precaution of sleeping apart from the mare would not have saved Garrison's life if he had bedded down on the ground anywhere close by, for the Indians searched carefully. In the end they had to conclude that the horse was a stray, that her rider had come upon some misfortune elsewhere.

Garrison heard the Apaches leave at dawn, laughing and joking in delight over their unexpected prize. Garrison did not lift his head so that he could watch them go, nor did he come down from his niche.

The prickling sensation of danger stayed with him long after the rough humor of the Apaches and the morning prancing of their ponies had dwindled away in the distance.

He stayed in his hiding place all day. It was invisible from below, but it was naked to the sky and the bright brass plate of the pitiless sun. Through the day Garrison's thirst became steadily more intense. His lips became swollen and cracked, his tongue thick, his throat parched and dry. He could not have said for certain what hunch kept him where he was, his flesh frying on the skillet of burning rock, but stay there he did, stoically enduring his thirst, through the long hot day. He was close enough to the spring to hear its trickle. By nightfall the sound had become an obsession. He chased the watery vision in his mind, unable to stop tormenting himself.

Cool darkness brought some relief to his burning flesh, but the soft gurgle of water over rock continued through the night. He did not sleep.

In the haze of early morning the following day Garrison heard the last of the Apaches mount up and ride away. This time he risked a look. The Indian was alone, and he was riding Garrison's mare. Presumably he had claimed her as the price for staying behind in the hope of surprising her rider.

Garrison rose from his narrow perch, brought his rifle to his shoulder and dropped the Apache with a single shot. The Indian, himself sensing danger, was whirling about when Garrison's bullet caught him in the throat.

Caution had its limits. It did not include letting yourself be turned loose in the desert without a horse. Survival often meant knowing when to be careful and when to take a risk.

Now, staring out at the snowbound land surrounding the soddy, Garrison knew that the prickly warning that had kept him waiting on that rock pan through a day and night of torture was repeating itself, but he could not see why.

He bundled up in his sheepskin-lined jacket and pulled on his gloves before stepping outside. His six-shooter he stuffed under his waistband to be warmed by his body, protected by his coat from the cold. He carried his rifle in his left hand, breeching it to place a bullet in the chamber before he opened the door.

The air was crisp and cold, but he had felt worse. The stillness was in sharp contrast with the blustery storm of the previous day. The breeze, though steady, was not strong. A howler would pile this powder snow ten feet deep where it drifted. The sky was cloudless overhead, with only a line of cotton piled against the eastern horizon breaking the blue immensity. The bottom of that cotton layer was burning, catching the first fire of dawn.

Garrison glanced at the ridge overlooking the canyon to the north and the cluster of buildings where he stood. Could a wolf on that promontory be mistaken for a man on horseback even in poor light? It seemed unlikely. Still, tired eyes might make such a mistake, or a fancy exaggerated by loneliness and fear might trick the senses.

Plodding through knee-deep snow, Garrison circled toward the corral, his gaze scanning the pure white drifts for any kind of mark. The sense of uneasiness was still with him. His thoughts kept coming back to that ghost on the rim.

Near the corral he found the tracks, and his face, already tight with cold, relaxed in a grin.

They were wolf tracks for sure. A loner, and he had indeed come from the direction of the bluff. Garrison could not see where the single line of tracks began—for that he would have to follow them back to the rise of the land—but there was no doubt of their origin. A lone wolf, big by the depth of his prints in the fresh snow, and hungry enough to skirt close to human habitation.

Contrary to what some men argued, Garrison knew that a wolf, even a lone wolf, would attack a man if he was hungry enough, but only if he was convinced that his prey was weak and vulnerable. He would shy away at the first hint of real danger.

This wolf was old enough to have learned the cost of recklessness. His tracks led toward the barn, then veered away abruptly. He had smelled horses there, or heard them, and his brand of caution had overcome his hunger. Where there were horses there were men. Men with guns.

Garrison followed the tracks a short distance past the barn, until he could see where they retreated into the distance and were lost to view. Then he turned back to the barn.

The snow had drifted against the side of the building and he had to clear some of it away before he could open the door. He stacked his rifle against the wall and used both hands to pry the door open against the resisting snow.

Too late, the jingle of metal warned him. The sweaty smell of man assaulted his nostrils in the same instant.

He tried to duck clear. The descending blow of an axletree caught him across the shoulder, a trailing length of chain biting into his neck. The glancing blow knocked him sprawling.

On his back Garrison clawed for the six-gun under his coat. Out of the darkness of the barn a burly figure lunged toward him. The wooden club swung down again, exploding against his skull.

~~~ 4 ~~~

Within the soddy the silence was absolute. For a full minute after she woke Trish Lovell could not explain why this silence seemed wrong. She lay staring at the blanket shielding her sleeping alcove, wondering why she had drawn it over an empty room.

Then she remembered.

She sat up abruptly. The blankets, falling from her shoulders, exposed her to the morning chill. Had the fire gone out? she wondered as she scrambled out of bed. Garrison had banked it before he slept, working with thoughtful care. At the time she could not help thinking of Virgil Pryor's indifferent acceptance of her responsibility for everything about the house, cooking and sweeping and tending to the fire. Indifferent, that is, until she allowed the fire to go out on a cold night.

Trish dressed hastily, wondering if Garrison was still asleep. She could not hear his breathing now, and when she had awakened once during the night it had been quite audible. She had been a long time getting back to sleep.

She was aware of a confusion in her feelings. One minute she was remembering the bitter despair of her teenage years, after the death of her parents and what she had viewed as Garrison's abandonment of her. The next minute she was eagerly reaching for the blanket curtain, anticipating her first glimpse of him, glad that he had reappeared at last, if only for a night, a day.

The soddy—with the curtain drawn a single room again —was empty.

Trish Lovell checked her disappointment, noting that his blanket had been folded neatly by his roll. That neatness with his gear had surprised her eight years ago, she recalled. She had not expected it in a man wandering alone over a rugged frontier. It had taken her a while to understand that there was a sensible reason for his tidiness. He was not a fussy man. He simply dealt with reality. A roll that was not tied properly might come loose during a long ride. A mug that was not put immediately with the rest of his gear when it was empty could too easily be forgotten—and he did not carry a spare. A gun that was not kept clean and oiled might fail when it was needed.

The fire that he had carefully banked had not gone out, but it was burning low. Shivering, she quickly added wood to the coals. Then she went to the window.

She saw his tracks instantly. They were the only signs of life in the silent white wilderness that greeted her.

They made a line toward the corral before veering toward the barn. He had walked beyond the barn for some reason, then retraced his steps. The barn door stood slightly open, confirming the evidence of his tracks through the snow.

That was like him too, she thought. The first thing he had always done at the end of a ride, or upon waking in the morning, was to see to his horse. She wondered, with a quick nostalgic hope, if he still rode the same black horse he had had eight years ago, the horse she had come to know so well and even to love with a child's quick devotion.

She drew on a rebozo, a gift Ramon Sanudo had brought back from one of his unpredictable trips, and left the cabin briefly for her morning toilet, hurrying to the small, lean-to shelter a short distance from the soddy.

When she returned to the house Garrison had not yet appeared from the barn. She was smiling when she re-entered the snug warmth of the soddy. She felt unexpectedly cheerful. The morning had a purpose missing from so many recent mornings. She was glad of something to do, someone to cook for, activity to fill the emptiness of another day. She found a potato and an onion in the cellar, hesitated only an instant over what was nearly the last of the bacon, and began to prepare breakfast.

The shelter was soon filled with the smells of bacon and onion and heating coffee. She warmed some leftover bread to soften it, humming to herself. Garrison should be back from the barn shortly. If not she would have to call him out.

She was lifting the bacon from the pan when she heard the door scrape open. Smiling, she speared the last slice with a long fork before she turned with a feeling of anticipation toward the door.

A startled gasp broke from her lips. Fork and bacon

slipped from her hand to fall on the hearth, and her heart thudded with alarm.

A stranger stood in the doorway. A burly man with a black stubble of beard, broad flat features, small dark eyes set wide apart so that he reminded her of a wolf. The rifle held in his hands was pointing casually toward her.

"Well now," he said with a grin like a snarl, "it looks like I come just in time for breakfast!"

CHAPTER 3

~~~ 1 ~~~

There were three of them. Shouldering into the low-ceilinged soddy, they brought with them a breath of cold and a feeling of dread that Trish Lovell could not shake.

The sight of Garrison shocked her. He was draped over the shoulder of the biggest of the three strangers, carried like a sack of grain. The big man dumped Garrison onto the floor. He fell in a heap and did not move. Trish was certain that he was dead. The sight of his face sickened her. The entire left side of his face was swollen and discolored, an ugly blue, streaked with blood where the cheek had split open.

The men ignored Garrison. They ordered her to finish putting onto the table the breakfast she had been preparing for herself and Garrison. They bolted the food down hungrily. Then the apparent leader, the black-bearded man who had first appeared at her door and was called Staggs, demanded that she fry the remainder of the bacon and more potatoes. They ate the last of the bread as well.

While they ate, speaking little beyond grunts of satisfaction, Garrison gave a groan that told her for the first time that he was alive. She kept staring at him, hardly able to take her eyes from the ugly swelling of his cheek, her mind filled with anxiety. How badly was he hurt? And who were these men? Why had they attacked Garrison?

Staggs took note of her distraught concern. "He'll live," Staggs said. "And maybe wish he hadn't."

"Why are you doing this?" she burst out. "Who are you?"

Staggs' small, wide-spaced eyes held neither pity nor interest in her questions. "We'll talk soon enough," he said. "Suppose you make some more coffee. And this time put some grounds in it. We didn't ask for tea."

The next time Trish looked at Garrison his eyes were open. They had a dull, blurred look, but a few minutes later he was sitting up, alert, his back propped against the soddy's front wall. He studied the three strangers bleakly. An expression she took for anger was, in fact, self-disgust. That prowling wolf had been smarter than he was. The critter had not been scared off by the presence of horses in the barn. He had smelled man. His tracks had told a story Garrison felt he should have been able to read.

Finally he spoke. "Now you've filled your bellies, mind tellin' me who you are and what this is all about?"

"Staggs is the name," the black-bearded man said. He was clearly the spokesman for the trio. "The big one is called Cullen, and that good-lookin' waddy there is Dandy." He grinned at Trish Lovell. "Dresses like a dude, but don't let that fool you."

"I suppose you got a reason for poleaxing me—"

"You're the one's got some explainin' to do," Staggs said, cutting off Garrison's comment. "Now, we been nice and polite, told you who we was. Suppose you do the same."

Garrison's eyes narrowed, but his battered face was otherwise expressionless. "Garrison," he said shortly. "And the woman is—" He hesitated, his glance touching hers.

Staggs continued to grin. "Mrs. Pryor," he said softly.

He looked from Garrison to her and back. "Ol' Virg Pryor's missus, that's who she is. Maybe you'd like to tell us how come you're rollin' up your blankets under Virg Pryor's roof, you and Mrs. Pryor all cozy together."

There was a stillness in the room. Staggs kept grinning, but there was a meanness to the expression. It had nothing to do with humor. Garrison looked at the three men in turn, all watching him with an odd eagerness, as if his explanation for his presence there in the Pryor house was important to them in a way he could not guess.

He remembered talk about three badmen who had passed through Cedar Point a day or so ago. They had a smell about them, Raymond Soule had told Garrison. The smell of trouble. For a town man Soule had a good nose for trouble.

You couldn't tell much about a man in the West from what he wore, especially in winter. And most men smelled some when they had worn the same long underwear, the same jeans and shirt, often the same socks, for weeks at a time, all the while sitting a horse or working around cattle, sometimes not feeling the touch of bath water from first snow to spring thaw. What Soule had sensed was something that went beyond dirt or sweat. Meanness had its own aura.

For all his smiling, Staggs was a cold, dangerous man. His black, restless eyes were angry. They looked out at the world as if they felt cheated. They were the eyes of a man who had seen others prosper while he went hungry, and who meant to get even, one way or another.

Staggs was the *honcho* of the bunch, but it was Garrison's hunch that the small, lean man he had called Dandy was a snake with a deadlier bite. Beneath the heavy jacket he had shucked off he wore shiny black pants and boots, a matching black gunbelt with silver buckle and adornment on the holster, a fancy blue shirt with white

piping and pearl snap buttons. He didn't smile and he
wasted few words. His glance had licked over the comely
young woman in the room with obvious interest, but for
the rest of the time his gaze had almost never left Garrison. Dandy had white, long-fingered hands, the hands of
a gambler—or a gunman. Garrison guessed that anyone
who invested in so much expensive leather about his
waist prized his gun more than a deck of cards.

The third man, Cullen, was huge, meaty, with small,
dumb blue eyes punched into fat cheeks like raisins in
dough. A follower, Garrison thought, slow-witted, capable of the mindless cruelty of children, easily led by
someone with more intelligence and the same cruel
streak, like Staggs.

"When you're done lookin' us over," Staggs said, "I'm
still waitin' to hear about you and Mrs. Pryor. I reckon ol'
Virg would like to hear you tell it, too."

Garrison glanced at him sharply. "What do you have to
do with Pryor?"

"That's for me to know and you to wonder," Staggs retorted. He chuckled, as if the answer had been a clever
one. Dandy laughed appreciatively, and Cullen, watching
his two companions, took his cue and smiled eagerly, his
big head nodding. "You ain't in no position to ask questions, Garrison. But I'll be givin' you your answer soon
enough. First off, you're gonna tell us what you're doin'
here." His expression became sly. "Ol' Virg tell you to
look after his woman for him, did he?"

Garrison was tempted to let them wonder, but he saw
that such stubbornness would only bring trouble sooner
and harder. It was going to come anyway, he knew. Time
might give him a better chance to deal with it. Anyway,
it was best to set them straight about his presence there.
If they had a quarrel with Virgil Pryor, they might
quickly lose interest in Pryor's wife and a passing drifter,

once they were certain that Pryor himelf was long absent.

"I don't know Pryor," he said. "Never heard of him before yesterday, when I learned that Patricia"—he hesitated only a flicker—"was Mrs. Pryor now."

"Patricia, is it? Well, now, that's a right pretty name." Staggs turned thoughtfully toward the woman, as did the others, Dandy taking time only for a quick, sliding appraisal before his gaze shifted back to Garrison. Even the fact that Garrison was unarmed, facing three armed men, did not make Dandy relax. Yes, he was the one who would have to be taken out first, Garrison thought. If the chance ever came.

"You and Patricia, you're old friends, is that it, Mr. Garrison?"

"We go back a good ways. To when she was just a tucker."

"Uh-huh. Tell me the truth, now, Garrison, do you and Virg go back a long spell, too?"

"I told you, I never—"

"I know what you said. Fact is, I don't believe you, Garrison. It don't make any kind of sense that ol' Virg would let another man look after his woman . . . unless maybe he was here for a damned good reason. Like, to look after things for Virg. Look after his woman and . . . other things. That about the size of it, Garrison?"

"I don't know ol' Virg," Garrison said quietly. "You can ask Mrs. Pryor. She'll tell you I just stopped by here yesterday. Just to . . . to see how she was getting on."

"Uh-huh. When was the last time you stopped by, Garrison?"

He frowned, seeing how his words were being twisted into lies. "It's been some years. Like I told you, I knew Mrs. Pryor when she was just a young'un. I happened along this way and I . . . I wanted to see her." The story sounded lamer and more implausible, it seemed, with each added explanation.

Staggs was grinning at him. He spoke to Trish Lovell without looking at her. "That the truth, Mrs. Pryor?"

"That's right. He's telling the truth." Her voice was steady. When Garrison had first awakened in the soddy, his head still swimming from the blow he had taken, he had glimpsed terror in her eyes. He didn't know if she was panicked by the sight of him with his battered face or by the three men who had so suddenly appeared out of nowhere. But now her nerves had calmed. If she was frightened, she managed to conceal it fairly well. "He doesn't know Virgil at all."

"Uh . . . how long's it been since Garrison come by the last time? It's been some years, he says. That right?"

"It's true. It's been . . . eight years."

"Eight years!" Staggs' awestruck tone mocked her. "You hear that, boys? Eight years, and then all of a sudden he rode through hell's own snow just to say hello. Would you ever have believed such a thing?"

Cullen looked unsure, but Dandy shook his head, smiling thinly. "She's a right pretty liar," he said.

"We're tellin' the truth!" Trish Lovell insisted hotly. "Anyway, what does it matter to you? Who are you? I never heard Virgil speak of any Dandy or Cullen or Staggs. What are you doing here?"

"Why, we're friends of ol' Virg, didn't I tell you that? We're kind of like Garrison here. We just stopped by to say hello, right, boys? We come maybe five hundred miles, near froze to the saddle, just to find Virgil's place, just so we could say hello."

"Well, you won't find him here," Trish declared. "He's been gone more'n two months, and I don't know when he'll be back."

"Is that a fact?" Staggs grinned his mean-eyed, mock-

ing grin. "And he left you here all alone, did he? Right
here in the middle of nowhere?"

"Yes, he—" She caught herself. "No, he didn't—he
wouldn't do that. But it wasn't Mr. Garrison he left with
me. We have two hands. . . ." She went on to explain
about Pegleg Parks' accident and about Ramon Sanudo's
absence. Even to Garrison the explanation had an im-
probable ring, and he saw that Staggs did not believe her
for a moment.

"I like a woman knows how to lie," Staggs said, deceptively amiable. "I reckon Virgil wouldn't ask his woman
to do any less. But it won't hold water, Mrs. Pryor."

"But I'm tellin' you the truth!" She was suddenly close
to tears.

Staggs shook his head sadly. "You got to do better than
that, ma'am. Now you surely are gonna tell us the truth,
and that's a fact, you and Garrison. But you ain't started
to tell it yet." His cold glance flicked toward Garrison.
"Now it's true enough he rode in here late yesterday,
'cause we watched him come in. But what we seen was,
he rode right in just like he owned the place. He knew
where he was headin', and he put his horse straight in the
barn like he knew exactly which stall she liked best. And
then he walked up to your door here and you let him in
straightaway. And he stayed, Mrs. Pryor. You and him,
under this roof, just the two of you. If'n what he said was
straight, and he hadn't seen hide nor hair of you for eight
years, nor you of him, why, it ain't likely you'd have just
opened your door to him like that, like he hadn't been
gone more'n a day or two, is it? You see my problem,
Mrs. Pryor? You see why I'm havin' such a hard time
believin' you?"

"Let her alone," Garrison said. "You won't listen to gos-
pel when you hear it. Maybe it's time you laid it out,

what it is you're after." He paused. "It's Pryor you want, I reckon."

Staggs pushed away from the table where he had been leaning and confronted Garrison, staying just out of reach in case Garrison tried to lunge for him. Dandy eased forward, alert for trouble, and the big man, Cullen, appeared uneasy. His huge hands opened and closed into fists.

Garrison was not yet ready for any reckless moves. His six-gun and rifle had been taken from him. Staggs wore the Colt stuffed under his waistband, and Dandy had set Garrison's Winchester against the wall near the door. Garrison knew that he would not get two steps across the room before being cut down. Dandy, he guessed, was snake-quick with a gun, and getting past Cullen would be like trying to swim around a logjam.

"You want to get right down to business, Garrison?"

"You're here for a reason. It would save time all around if you said what it is. But you might as well know you won't find Pryor here."

"You seem mighty sure of that, considerin' as you say you only rode in here yesterday like the snow, ridin' the wind."

"Mrs. Pryor told you he's been gone. I heard the same in town when I was askin' how to find this place." His eyes narrowed in speculation. "You must've heard the same, if you was askin' about Pryor in Cedar Point."

"How'd you know we was in Cedar Point?"

Garrison shrugged indifferently. "Ain't many other places you could find around here, if you was lookin' for someone to answer a few questions. Like where Virgil Pryor hung his hat."

Raymond Soule's comments about the three badmen should have alerted him, Garrison thought sourly. He had had warning enough. Soule's comments. Trish Pryor's talk about a ghost on the ridge. His own instinct putting him on edge this morning. Plenty of warning, but he had let himself be lulled by his first impression of those wolf tracks, and he had walked right into the iron tip of an axletree. He deserved to have his head knocked off, or worse.

The worse, he thought, was coming.

"You're a quick one with the answers, Garrison," Staggs said after a moment. "Only trouble is, you're a liar, and that's a fact. The little lady plays fast and loose with the truth, too. Like, for instance, callin' herself Mrs. Pryor. The way I hear it, Virgil never took her before no preacher, which don't surprise me none. I got no quarrel with that—I ain't much of a one for listenin' to no windy sermons myself. Now, I don't mind the lady lyin' to me, 'cause that's surely what ol' Virgil told her to do, and she's only bein' an obedient woman. But you, now, you're different. If you're lyin' for Virg, you might as well know I can't swallow it. It sticks in my craw, right here."

"What reason would I have to lie?" Garrison said.

Staggs' eyes widened in mock surprise. "Why, you know that, Garrison. The money, of course."

"Money?" Garrison stared at him, his jaw hanging open. Of course it had to be money. What else would have brought men such as these no-accounts trekking five hundred miles through winter storms to an isolated ranch? Not love or friendship or curiosity. Hate might do it, and he had been wondering if they had a grudge against Virgil Pryor strong enough to drive them so far. But for men like Staggs and his crew, greed was an even stronger passion than hate.

"What money?" he repeated, covering the jolt of understanding.

Staggs lashed out suddenly, the back of his hand slamming across Garrison's swollen cheek with brutal force, rocking his head and bringing him halfway to his feet. But Staggs stepped quickly back out of reach, and a gun appeared in Dandy's hand.

"You damned well know what I'm talkin' about, Garrison. You'll tell us, you or the little lady. You can spill it out now, right off, and save us all a lot of trouble, or you can make us grind it out of you. I don't much care which way it happens. We got all the time in the world, and you got no place to go." His malevolent glare shifted from Garrison to the woman. "So which one of you is gonna tell it? Where's the money ol' Virgil stole?"

2

"Maybe you don't know everythin' there is to know about the money, and maybe you do. I can see that Virgil might not tell you any more'n he had to. He wouldn't trust anybody out of sight, seein' as he ain't one to be trusted himself. But you'll know, one or both of you, where Virgil might put something he wanted to hide. You got to know that much, or there wouldn't be any sense in him havin' you here to look after it."

Listening to him, Garrison recognized the uncomplicated logic in Staggs' reasoning, and in spite of himself he glanced wonderingly at Trish Lovell. She was frowning at Staggs, her expression merely puzzled. Could she feign such innocence? Garrison shook off the question irritably.

He wished that he knew more about Pryor—and about Trish Lovell's relationship with him. Her sketch of a reckless, charming, smiling man had revealed little of him that could be relied on. And even during that brief account Garrison had suspected she was holding back.

"You're staking a claim to that money?" he asked Staggs. "It's yours?"

"Well, now, you could say it was ours after we took it," Staggs said with his meaningless grin. "You want to know how it happened, Garrison? I'll tell you that much, just so's you'll see why there ain't no use you tryin' to hold out on us." He hooked a toe around the leg of a wooden chair and dragged it closer. He straddled the chair, facing its spoked back and folding his arms across the top. "We run onto Virgil more'n a year ago. That is, me and Cullen did. Dandy hooked up with us later on, and the four of us figgered out a way to make us some money. Virgil, he's a good one at figgerin' things out. We hit us a couple of stages, and then we started lookin' for bigger things, like maybe a bank or—"

"That's a lie!" Trish Lovell burst out. "Virgil isn't a thief!"

Staggs grinned at her amiably. "Maybe he didn't tell you where he found his money, ma'am, but he didn't pick it up off no porch stoop, and you can believe me he didn't punch cows for it. That ain't Virgil's way, Mrs. Pryor. You got to know him well enough for that."

"I don't . . . I don't believe you." She tried to make the assertion firmly, but her conviction was shaky. Her face had paled, and Garrison saw that Staggs' words had disturbed her. He wondered on how many previous occasions Pryor had disappeared for weeks or months at a time, leaving her alone, and if she had any idea where he went or what he did while he was gone.

"Virgil figgered a way for us to hit this cattleman's bank up Kansas way, and then how we could get away without bein' caught or even suspicioned."

"That took some figuring," Garrison said dryly.

"It surely did," Staggs agreed.

"All this talk ain't gettin' us anywheres," Dandy said suddenly.

Everyone looked at him, surprised at the interruption. Staggs grinned. "That's Dandy for you," he said. "Now, I'm not the most patient man in the world. You got to understand that, the both of you. But compared to Dandy I'm like Job hisself, and that's a fact. We'll get to it, Dandy, don't you worry about that."

"You robbed this bank?" Garrison asked. He wanted to keep Staggs talking, and he wanted to learn as much as possible, not only about the three men he faced but also about Pryor. Pryor was the key to the predicament in which he now found himself.

"Yeah, we robbed it," Staggs said.

"You shouldn't be tellin' him that!" Dandy objected.

Staggs feigned surprise. "Why not? Mr. Garrison ain't much of a talker. He wouldn't be workin' for ol' Virgil if he was the kind to go runnin' to the nearest lawman when he heard such a thing. That right, Garrison?"

"I told you I don't work for Pryor."

"I know what you told me. I also know you're here. Anyways," Staggs went on, "Virgil worked it out when there was a lot of money in that bank. There had to be 'cause there was one drive just come in from down Texas way, and others was movin' that direction to the railroad. Virgil picked this Saturday night to do it, when the town was noisy and full of trailhands celebratin'. There was no way we'd be noticed, you see. The town was so full of whiskey-soaked hands you couldn't go down an alley without trippin' over one or another."

"That sounds dangerous," Garrison said thoughtfully. "You had a ready-made posse there to chase you."

"That was the slick part of it," Staggs said with a grin. "I told you Virgil was slick as an eel. We hit that bank around midnight, goin' in through the back door. The money was in this safe, but Cullen here, he blew it open like it was a can of beans. You wouldn't think it, maybe, him bein' so big, but he's good with his hands and he can handle dynamite real good. We was in and out of that bank fast, and there must've been twenty-five thousand dollars in those money sacks, Garrison. That was a mistake Virgil made, 'cause he reckoned there'd be more, but that was the only mistake he made. We had our horses waitin' out back, and before the dust settled inside that bank and the town could come runnin', we was ridin' hell for leather for the hills."

"What about the posse?" Garrison asked curiously. "How did you get away?"

Staggs chuckled. "Why, that posse chased after us for three whole days before they give up. I know that for a fact, 'cause we was in that posse." He paused to savor Garrison's look of astonishment. "That's right. Dandy and Cullen and me, we was all deputized. But not Virgil. We was chasin' him."

Garrison frowned. "I don't understand."

"Nobody else figgered it out either," Staggs said. "It worked just the way Virgil planned it. You see, we had three horses waitin' just a mile out of town. Dandy and Cullen and me, we switched horses and circled straight back to the town. We got there while the marshal was still tryin' to round up some deputies to go huntin' for the bank robbers. But Virgil, he lit a shuck. He had the money, and he had four horses. You see, that's how come the posse never did catch up to him. He'd ride the legs off one horse, and then he jumped on the next one. He kept doin' that, and the posse couldn't keep up. We only had the horses we were ridin', and by the second day they was wore out. Come the third day and even that marshal knew it was no use goin' on. We found a couple of the horses Virgil left behind. One of 'em was dead and the other was near to it. By that time the marshal had tumbled to it that we wasn't chasin' four men, like he'd thought all along, but only one or two. He couldn't figger out what happened to the others. Virgil got away clean. There was no way the posse could keep up with him when he had four horses to ride in turn and the riders in that posse only had one horse to a man." Staggs shook his head admiringly, but after a moment his grin faded. "Only thing is, Virgil just kept on runnin', and he had all the money."

"Weren't you supposed to meet him somewhere? You must have had some such plan."

"Why, sure, Garrison. We had that planned. But the three of us had to wait, you can see that. We had to go back with the posse and hang around a spell, so's nobody would wonder where we went all of a sudden. We waited a couple of weeks, and let it be heard that we had to head back to Texas. There was so many trail hands around from different outfits, each one must've thought we were with another one. We drifted out when it was safe, but Virgil, he'd had two weeks by that time to get lost. We was supposed to rendezvous over in New Mexico and divvy up the money. Trouble is, Virgil never showed up there. It took a while before we caught on that he'd slickered us, just like he slickered that town. He never meant for us to get our share."

"I don't believe a word of this," Trish Lovell said.

"Now, ma'am, what reason would I have to tell you a tale? No reason at all."

"When did this happen?" Garrison asked. "Pryor hasn't been here since September, Mrs. Pryor says, so he couldn't have hidden the money here since then."

"Yeah, but he was here in August. That right, Mrs. Pryor?" Staggs demanded sharply.

"Yes, he was here—" She broke off, realizing that she

had been trapped into an admission. "He was only here a week or so, and then he had to . . . to go north."

"Uh-huh. We robbed that bank first week in August. He had time to get here and hide the money, that's for sure. He wouldn't have buried it in the desert, that's the way I see it. He'd have taken it where it would be safe, where somebody could keep an eye on it. Then he taken off again. It's my guess he went south, not north. He didn't want to run into us, his good friends that he double-crossed."

"Maybe he wasn't able to keep that meeting in New Mexico," Garrison suggested thoughtfully. "It doesn't make sense he'd steal from his partners when they knew where to find him. Why would he hide anything here when he knew this was where you'd look for him?"

"He didn't know that," Staggs answered, the meanness more evident as he reflected on Pryor's duplicity. "He never told us where he lived, or even that he had a place of his own. He'd tell us he was from St. Louis one time, or that he'd been up to Cheyenne, or that he just moved along from one place to the next."

"How did you track him here?"

"A man leaves tracks, Garrison, even when he don't want to. Even a smart man like Virgil. Folks notice him, and they remember little things. Virgil always wore these Mexican spurs, like a Texan does. That kinda pointed us this way. Then there was his boots. One time when Virgil was in town havin' a bath, Dandy had a look at his boots. They was fine boots and Dandy has an eye for such. Those boots had the maker's name stamped inside. They was made over in Fort Worth. So that's where we went huntin', and we kinda used our noses to get from Fort Worth over to Cedar Point." He paused, sullen eyes remembering the hard months of tracking. "It don't matter how we found this place, Garrison. But we found it.

We tracked Virgil all this way. It took us since September to do it, but we got here. And you have to understand one thing. You listen to me, too, Mrs. Pryor. Listen good. We didn't come all this way just to come up empty."

"Well, you have," Trish Lovell said defiantly. "Even if what you say is true, and I don't know why I should believe you at all, there's no money here."

Staggs stared at her. "It's here. It's got to be." The frustration of being hoodwinked out of his share of money he regarded as dearly earned was in his stubborn assertion. For a moment longer he brooded on Virgil Pryor's betrayal. Then he turned abruptly to his partners. "Dammit, Virgil wouldn't hide that money too far away! Start takin' this place apart. I'll watch these two. There was three big sacks of that money. He couldn't stuff 'em into no crack, so they shouldn't be so hard to find." He glared in the direction of the sleeping alcove. "Start with that bed. I don't care what you have to bust up—just find that money!"

～ 3 ～

Cullen and Dandy took nearly an hour to exhaust every possible hiding place in the soddy and its cellar, including digging holes all over the cellar and inspecting every part of the main room, ripping up the floorboards and running a pole up the chimney. Nothing.

The search moved to the barn. Here it was as destructive and impatient as the combing of the soddy. All three men took turns searching or watching Garrison and Trish Lovell, both of whom had been brought to the barn. Staggs even had Cullen shovel out the horse stalls and poke around in the adjoining corral. The deep snow made any outside search haphazard at best.

It had not seemed to occur to any of the three bank robbers that the most logical place for Pryor to have buried his stolen money, simply because it was the safest, was in the ground, marked in some way only he could know. The frozen earth made any such hole as safe as a vault until spring came with its softening ways.

Predictably, as the search wore on into the afternoon, its first frenzied prying and digging and smashing turned into frustrated bickering. The searchers cursed more angrily over each new failure, each new inspiration that proved false. In keeping with their increasingly sullen mood, the sky began to darken in midafternoon and the wind picked up. The blowing snow added to the gloom and cold.

Trish Lovell, on Staggs' instructions, had been allowed a coat, but Garrison had been hustled out to the barn without any winter cover. Since he had not been used during the search, the lack of activity and deepening cold let the chill seep into his bones.

Garrison knew what was coming before it happened. He could see the idea forming as the fruitless search wore on and the men's nerves frayed. He could see it in Dandy's sullen resentment and in Staggs' lengthening silences, the absence of even that pretense of a grin.

When they had exhausted everything else, there would be only Garrison left. And the woman. Garrison had no doubt they would use any means to get what they wanted.

Finally Staggs called a halt to the destruction of the barn. As the group trooped across the yard toward the house through drifting snow, Garrison studied the dark sky to the north. Another pod of the storm was moving in. Darkness would come early, shortening the day. Dark, he thought, was his only possible ally.

When they were in the house and had done with

stomping snow from their boots and shedding their heavy coats, the three badmen held a low-voiced confab. Staggs turned away to confront Dave Garrison.

His words were a surprise. "I've got a proposition to make you, Garrison."

Garrison's surprise showed only briefly in a narrowing of his eyes. He stood with his back to the fireplace, luxuriating in the feeling of having the cold baked out of him. His hands, he suspected, were close to being frostbitten. "What might that be?" he drawled calmly.

"I'm bettin' that Pryor promised you a share of that money. A small share, if I know Virgil. And I'll eat dirt if he told you how much there was."

"Go on."

"You show us where that money is and we'll vote you in for a full share. Now what do you say to that?"

Garrison refrained from smiling. Staggs had to think him even more a fool than he had showed himself to be. For a moment he was silent. Finally he started to reach for his shirt pocket and checked the move. "Okay if I make a smoke?"

"What's that got to do with our offer?"

"Helps me think," Garrison said.

Staggs glared at him. "Go ahead. But be careful how you reach for the makin's. Slow and easy, so's I can watch your hands."

Garrison formed a cigarette carefully, twisted one end and, as if he had just remembered her presence, glanced at Trish Lovell. "You don't mind?" he asked politely.

"No, I don't mind." She watched him light the cigarette with a match and draw in a long pull of smoke. Virgil Pryor wouldn't have asked, she thought.

Watching Garrison, the long lean body relaxed now, slack and no longer shivering, as if he hadn't a worry in the world, his gaze steady and thoughtful as he appeared to ponder Staggs' proposal, she realized that she didn't know him at all. Not really. The girl who had fallen in love with him hadn't known him either—or herself. She had only thought she loved him, exaggerating feelings of gratitude and admiration and a girl's lonely yearning. But the sense of betrayal when he rode off alone had been real and painful. It was a feeling she had never forgotten, and it had changed her. In the long run, in the way of things, it had even turned her to look for someone else, another man, someone flashing and exciting, better than a faded memory. Someone like Virgil Pryor.

She wondered if Garrison felt any fear at all. None showed. But what did he hope to accomplish by pretending to consider a revelation he could not make?

"Well?" Staggs demanded impatiently. "You've had time enough."

"I been doin' a lot of thinking all day," Garrison said. "While you've been huntin' for that missing money. Thinking about Pryor mostly. Now I don't know the man"—he held up a hand to forestall Staggs' angry interruption—"like I told you, I never met him, but I've learned some things about him, just listening. For one thing, I know he wouldn't hide that loot where anyone could come along and find it easy. If it's here at all, it's buried. And there's no way anyone will find it before greenup."

"Damn you—"

"Another thing," Garrison went on, riding over Staggs' outburst, "you ought to know he wouldn't trust me or anyone else to know where the money is. Even if I was workin' for him, like you been thinking, do you really believe he'd trust me any more than he'd leave you alone with that money?"

Staggs' voice was deceptively soft as he said, "That's what you been thinkin', is it?"

"It makes sense," Garrison drawled.

"You're a smooth-talkin' sonuvabitch. You believe him, Dandy?"

"He's a liar all the way. Both of 'em are."

"What about you, Cullen? You reckon we should take Mr. Garrison at his word, tuck in our tails and ride away, and forget all about that money of ours?"

Scowling on cue, Cullen shook his massive head. He flexed his hands. They were like loaves of bread. "No. He shouldn't lie."

"What do you do with a man who lies to you like that?"

Cullen stared at him uncertainly.

"Why, you do what you do with anyone who's bad. You take him out behind the barn and teach him a lesson." Staggs grinned maliciously. "Garrison's been gettin' warm as toast there by that fire. Maybe he'll remember better if he's cooled off some. Take him out by the barn and see if you can't persuade him to right his ways. Stay where we can see you. And Cullen"—Staggs paused, looking at Garrison and the woman—"don't kill him. I want him alive, understand? Cullen? You hear what I'm sayin'?"

The big man's eyes were eager, more alive than Garrison had seen them before. "Yeah—I understand."

"Good. It's okay if he's hurt some. It wouldn't be a good lesson if he didn't hurt. But I don't want him fixed so he can't talk when he's ready!"

4

Staggs was taking no chances. He sent Dandy out with Cullen and Garrison. The graceful little gunfighter carried a rifle, and he kept a careful distance from Garrison, alert for any attempt to run or pull a trick. Staggs watched from the doorway of the house, pushing Trish Lovell out in front of him and compelling her to watch.

She didn't want to. Reading the fear that widened her eyes, Staggs whispered in her ear, "You can stop it any time you want. All you got to do is tell me where it is."

"I don't know! Can't you understand that? I don't know anything about that money. Even if it's here, do you think Virgil would tell me? Mr. Garrison is right. Virgil isn't the kind to go off for all this time if *anyone* knew where that money was."

Staggs scowled. He had not given credence to the same argument from Garrison and he could not accept it from her. Stubbornly he shook his head. "It's got to be here. He came back here with it. He wouldn't have taken it with him after that. It wouldn't have been safe to carry it with him while he was gonna stay on the dodge. Besides, even if he wouldn't trust the likes of us, you're his woman."

"But Virgil wouldn't trust me!" she cried in desperation, in her anxiety revealing to herself more than she would have liked to admit, a truth about her relationship with Virgil Pryor that she had not faced before so squarely. That door, once opened, revealed more. "He doesn't care about anyone but himself, not that way."

"Shut up!" said Staggs angrily. "Maybe you just don't want to see Garrison busted up. I reckon maybe Virgil's got reason to suspicion you in some ways. But you had to see that money when he come back with it. You got to know it's here. If you don't know for sure where it's hidden, you can make some damned good guesses."

"Oh my God!" she whispered, staring toward the barn.

Garrison had not waited to take his punishment. He broke out of Cullen's grasp near the barn. Trying to elude the big man, Garrison slipped on the snow, staggered, and stumbled within reach of Cullen's hands. Cullen picked him up as if he were a child and threw him against the wall of the barn. The crack of flesh and bone against the wood was as solid as the blow of an ax.

Garrison sagged toward the ground. Cullen closed in again, surprisingly quick for a man of his size, but this time the slippery footing worked against him. His feet went out from under him and he sat in the snow.

Garrison was up first, his back against the barn wall as if for support. Cullen lumbered to his feet and charged. Garrison let him start a wild swing and used the wall to push himself away from the blow. A huge fist whistled past his head as he ducked clear. He tried a kick at Cullen's kneecap as the big man went by, but the uncertain footing made the kick awkward and it missed.

In any other circumstances the fight would have been even more of a mismatch, but it soon became clear that the snow and icy ground beneath it worked against Cullen more than Garrison. Heavy and ponderous, Cullen built up a full head of steam when he charged, and it was hard for him to stop or change direction, especially when he would start to slip and slide. On his next bearlike lunge Garrison skipped out of the way and slammed a fist into Cullen's side as he went by. When the big man skidded as he whirled around, Garrison hit him again.

The solid blows, however, had no effect. Cullen lumbered after him.

Twice more Garrison eluded the bear, but then his boots went skating on an icy patch and Cullen was able to corner him between the barn wall and the half-open door. He looked around for a way out as Cullen closed in.

Dandy's rifle cracked once. The shot was not meant to hit, but it stopped Garrison short. He hesitated an instant too long. Cullen's fist smashed into his face, and he went down as if he had been clubbed.

Even from across the yard Trish Lovell could see the bright red that spattered the snow and made a smear of Garrison's face. She moaned involuntarily and looked away, unable to bear the sight. Staggs jerked her head around, forcing her to look again.

"You want to see him alive," Staggs hissed in her ear, "you'll talk!"

He pulled her through the doorway and flung her into the house.

CHAPTER 4

~~~~ 1 ~~~~

The day slid almost imperceptibly into night. It was not yet five o'clock, Garrison reckoned, but the black mass of the storm completely blotted out the sun.

Encased in cold as if inside a block of ice, Garrison shivered uncontrollably, and his teeth made an audible clicking. His fingers were numb, but he could not be sure if they were frostbitten or had lost all sensation from having the circulation cut off. The rope binding his wrists had been jerked so tight that it had bitten into the flesh. His legs were hobbled at the ankles, and a short length of rope tied him to a corral post that butted against a corner of the barn.

Periodically he worked his fingers and his toes, trying to stave off the inevitable. After a while, when the snow drifting across the yard before the gusting winds began to pile higher against the barn, he found that he could knee enough of it into shape to form a kind of cave. There he huddled for some protection against the cutting wind.

If they waited much longer, he thought, they would need a pick to chip him loose.

He was beyond pain. He had been this cold before, but never helpless before it. To take his mind from that helplessness he set puzzles to be solved. The puzzle of Virgil Pryor. If you were Pryor, would you bury your money here and then disappear? Maybe. A man as cunning as

Pryor seemed to be would figure that he might be tracked this far. He wouldn't stay to be surprised as Garrison had been surprised. But he might well leave his stolen money behind. He wouldn't bury it in the desert but in a place he knew, a place he could be sure of returning to and finding it the same.

The puzzle of Patricia Lovell Pryor. *Did she know?*

And, finally, the puzzle of Dave Garrison and the whim that had brought him to this bitter end, trussed up like a chicken in a hollow as cold as a grave.

A sound jerked Garrison's head up. He peered out of his snow cave, eyes straining to make out meaningful shapes. Had a shadow moved there, beyond the empty corral?

A tumbleweed broke past the poles at the north side of the corral and rolled lightly across the snow until it came up against the side of the barn.

Garrison's eyes watered. He sank back into his hollow, blinking. His head began to nod toward his chest.

He didn't see the door to the soddy open. They were coming across the yard toward him when his head lifted. He saw one of the men pull the door shut, erasing that rectangle of light. Then they were only dark shapes, thick under their heavy coats, plodding through the snow.

Staggs loomed over him. He kicked Garrison's snowbank down, exposing him more to the wind. "Where is the money, Garrison? You ready to tell us now?"

His lips felt like boards. He couldn't move them.

"Damn it, man, is it worth dyin' for? Money that ain't even your own?"

Garrison shook his head, but Staggs misunderstood the gesture. He reached down suddenly to pull Garrison's head back by the hair. "You won't talk to save your own hide. I can see that. But what about her?"

"I can't tell you. . . ." Garrison mumbled.

Staggs released him. "Dandy! Take her into the barn—just you and her. And don't get so far away we can't hear you. I want Garrison to hear her yell."

Dandy stepped forward eagerly to seize Trish Lovell by the arm. She tried to twist free, but the slender gunfighter held her easily. He dragged her toward the barn door. Garrison could not see her face clearly, but he heard the silent struggle.

"No!" he said. The sound was a croak. "All right, you win! I'll tell you."

Staggs was bending close in an instant, grinning with triumph. "Where? It's here, ain't it? I knew it!"

Garrison tried to talk but the words wouldn't come. His head slumped forward. He felt Staggs pulling at him, heard his voice suddenly anxious, but the sound was far away.

Then there were hands under his arms, lifting him. He felt the rope fall away from his ankles. His wrists were still tied together but he was on his feet, Cullen supporting him, surprisingly gentle.

They hurried him across the yard. Moments later Garrison felt the shock of warmth as he was dragged into the soddy.

~ 2 ~

They cut the frozen rope away from his wrists. In a few minutes there were hot needles of pain in his hands and fingers. He was grateful for it. The pain revived him, and it told him that he had not frozen as badly as he had feared. Not yet.

"If this is another stunt," Staggs said, "you're a dead man, Garrison. You hear me?"

He nodded. His gaze found Trish Lovell across the room, white-faced, eyes despairing. He thought: *No, she doesn't know. Pryor wouldn't tell her.*

He looked bleakly at Staggs. "Pryor will kill me when he finds out."

"He won't get the chance," Staggs retorted. "Not unless you talk now. You ain't got much of a choice, Garrison. Maybe you can run from Pryor . . . but we're here now. Where did he hide that money?"

"You could just about reach up and touch it."

Involuntarily Staggs and the others looked up. There was only the ceiling: a tight row of poles lashed together, supported by heavier crossbeams.

His gaze shot back to Garrison.

"Sod roof," Garrison said.

"What are you tryin' to tell me?" Staggs glanced upward again, this time with dawning comprehension. "Do you mean—?"

"He wanted it close by when he was here," Garrison said. "And close enough so's I'd know if anyone tried to get at those bags while Pryor was gone. The money's up top, buried about where the sod roof meets the back of the rise." He shrugged. "Ground's frozen now, I reckon."

Excitement grew behind Staggs' eyes, behind the mirthless twist of his lips. "That's him," he said softly. "That's ol' Virgil. That's just like him, hidin' that money right over our heads. He'd have a good laugh if he knew we was this close and never found it." The outlaw chuckled, and the chuckle grew into a roar of laughter in which Cullen and Dandy joined him. "Last laugh's on us, boys! Let's go get that money! Cullen, you go fetch a shovel. Dandy, you can help him."

Dandy's laughter cut off abruptly. "Why me?" he protested. "How come we're supposed to do all the work?"

"Somebody's got to watch these two."

"Cullen can dig that money up—he don't need me to hold his hand. Anyways, it's black as pitch out there and there must be a yard of snow up top. How are we supposed to know where we're diggin' through that in the dark?"

"You want your share?" Staggs asked grimly.

"It ain't gonna walk away if we wait till mornin', when we can see what the hell we're doin'."

Staggs was on the edge of an angry outburst but he checked himself. Dandy wasn't one to be pushed too hard, Garrison thought, even by Staggs.

Staggs thought about it a moment, pacing restlessly, his glance darting toward the roof as if he could somehow see past the barrier of poles to the bags of money so cleverly hidden just out of reach. The roof was lowest at the front, so low that men as tall as Garrison and Cullen had to stoop when coming through the doorway. It slanted upward to meet the hillside, the back portion of the soddy and the cellar being actually cut into the hill. The money wouldn't be buried on the lower part of the roof, Staggs thought, where any hump would be visible. Most likely it would be right there where the roof joined the lip of the slope—invisible to the eye, yet easy to get at.

Still, Dandy was right. It was dark and windy and cold, and the money wasn't going to get up and walk away.

"All right," he said finally. "We waited this long. We'll wait till mornin'."

~~~ 3 ~~~

During the next hour, while Trish Lovell cooked supper, Staggs, Cullen and Dandy were in good humor. They talked and joked about the money, working it out how much each of them would have as his share, how much more each would get with Virgil Pryor cut out of his original share. It would serve Pryor right for double-crossing his partners. Dandy was the only one who wished aloud that Pryor were there. Staggs laughed at him. "You're quick, Dandy," he said. "But ol' Virgil, he's like grease jumpin' in a hot pan. You better be glad he ain't here . . . and hope he don't catch up."

Dandy didn't like that. After a moment of bristling he said, "Maybe we should wait for him right here. I don't want him chasin' me, not knowin' when or where he might jump me."

The suggestion sobered the others, but even the prospect of Virgil Pryor's wrath could not subdue their jovial spirits for long. They started talking about what each would do with his money. Cullen was going to stick with Staggs, but Dandy thought he might head for California. A man ought to do something special with money like that, he said. He shouldn't wake up some morning and find it all gone, and wonder what he had enjoyed during the brief time he had it. Not Dandy. He was going to know what he had enjoyed.

Trish Lovell took advantage of their mood to spoon out a helping of stew and dumplings for Garrison and herself as well as the others. Staggs observed this but let it go. It was the first food Garrison had tasted in twenty-four hours and he went at it like a pig at a trough, devouring his portion before Staggs changed his mind.

The food and the warmth of the soddy slowly began to make him feel human again. He suspected that Cullen had broken his nose with that one solid blow. It was badly swollen and he had to breathe mostly through his mouth. He didn't like the color or the lingering numbness of one finger and the lobe of his left ear, but he counted himself lucky so far.

Except for Staggs' decision to wait until morning before sending the others up on the roof. If the weather cleared and they all came out to watch the digging, Garrison knew that he wouldn't have a chance.

After supper, warm and stuffed and satisfied, the three outlaws gradually fell silent. Garrison became aware of Staggs' steady, speculative stare. He wondered if Staggs was trying to decide when to kill him. Garrison had no doubt that the decision that he had to die had already been made. The only question was when.

Staggs wouldn't act until he had the money in his hands, Garrison thought.

Staggs had a long wait for that.

Dandy no longer watched Garrison as closely as he had during the day. His eyes were mostly on Trish Lovell now. The aborted promise at the barn, when Staggs had told him he could do what he wanted with the girl, had awakened the gunman's barely concealed lust. His eyes undressed her, greedily examining the swell of bosom, the dipping curve of waist and hip, the soft skin of her throat. . . .

Garrison saw that she was aware of Dandy's stare and that it frightened her. In the light of the oil lamp she looked drawn but prettier than ever, her long yellow hair catching the light like spun gold.

The silence in the room lengthened, stretching out to

an hour. At last Trish rose and went to the sleeping alcove. She started to draw the curtain and Staggs said, "Here! What do you think you're doin'?"

"I'm going to . . . I need some sleep."

"You don't need to hide behind a blanket for that."

"I can't sleep with a room full of men sitting there watching me!" she said defiantly.

Staggs regarded her without sympathy. "Maybe you got a reason for hidin'. Dandy, see if she's got a gun stashed away there somewhere."

With a quick grin Dandy moved to the sleeping alcove, his glance licking over the woman as he sidled past. He checked the bed, lifted and pummeled the thin mattress, probed into the corners. Since the bed had already been searched earlier in the day in the hunt for the missing money, Garrison doubted that Staggs had seriously expected to find a weapon. He was simply being careful.

Finally Dandy shrugged. "Ain't even a hatpin," he said. He licked his lips. "Maybe I ought to search her."

Trish's breath caught. There was a taut moment of silent waiting. Garrison eased forward, shifting his weight. Staggs caught the movement and scowled, his hand moving quickly to the gun at his waist. Then he said, with a nasty grin, "She wouldn't have no hideout gun."

"How do we know? Maybe she would—"

"You'll have your chance, Dandy," Staggs said curtly. It had crossed his mind that the money was not yet in his hands. Instinctive judgment told him he would have to kill Garrison if he let Dandy have his way now, and he didn't want Garrison permanently silenced until the buried money was found. "Yeah, you'll have your chance," he promised. "I figger ol' Virgil owes us more'n just that money."

When Dandy returned reluctantly to the main room Trish Lovell said, "Can I draw the curtain now?"

Her voice was steady. It reminded Garrison of that suddenly orphaned girl who had choked back grief and panic one terrible night eight years ago, when he had found her by the riverbank.

"No," Staggs decided. "I want you where I can see you."

Defeated, she withdrew to her bed, lying down clothed as she was and pulling a blanket over her before she turned her back to the room. The men all watched her for a while before losing interest—except Dandy.

The silence in the house was not an easy one. Staggs was restless. He rose frequently to check the fire, to peer out the window, to listen to the faint sounds of blowing snow outside. The wind came in gusts, carrying flurries of snowflakes, but the new storm had not yet brought any heavy fall. He sat again in the only chair, flicked a glance at the ceiling, and fell back to staring at Garrison.

"I don't like it," Staggs said suddenly.

Everyone came alert. Cullen had been dozing off, sitting on a bench and cradling his head on the table. He shook himself like a dog shedding water. The table trembled. Dandy, who had been watching the sleeping woman, eyed Staggs sharply. "What's wrong?"

"I don't like him sittin' there like he just filled his hand with aces," Staggs said, nodding toward Garrison. "How do we know he ain't still spinnin' us a tale? He could just be buyin' himself another night to live."

Dandy shrugged his thin shoulders. "Easy way to fix that."

"No—not till we're sure, one way or another. But he could be runnin' another bluff." Staggs pushed to his feet. "I want a look at that money tonight. It's clear enough out there for diggin'. Snow's almost stopped."

"Well, I told you, I ain't goin' up there to do any diggin' tonight," Dandy protested.

"You don't have to. Cullen can do it. That right, Cullen? You'd like to count your share of that money, wouldn't you?"

"Huh?" Cullen blinked slowly. "Yeah. Yeah, sure. I'll find it." He rose massively.

"Better not send him up there," Garrison said quietly.

"Why not?" Staggs demanded.

"Same reason you wouldn't run a herd across the roof. He'd likely come right through the ceiling. He's too heavy."

Staggs considered this, still suspicious. "Maybe. Maybe he is. But you're not too heavy, Garrison. And you know where that money's buried. You can do the digging. Dandy, you'll watch him to make sure he digs. Cullen, you can watch him, too—just stay back where it's solid. Don't go on the roof."

Dandy said, "I told you, I ain't goin' out there—"

Staggs turned on him in sudden, savage fury. "You'll go if you want your California stake!"

He was ready to challenge Dandy now. The little gunfighter jerked taut, quick anger flashing in his eyes. His gun hand hovered over the butt of his six-shooter. The moment waited only for another spark to set off the explosion.

Cullen's deep voice rumbled. "You better not."

Dandy's eyes flicked from Staggs to Cullen, examining this new threat. Cullen would always side with Staggs. Dandy believed that he could beat Staggs. He might even have time to put a bullet into Cullen as well, but the big man would still be able to reach him with those powerful hands. One bullet would not stop him.

Dandy eased back on his heels, relaxing, letting his gun hand drop casually to his side. "Okay, okay. But I still say it could wait until morning."

Staggs answered him bluntly. "Do it now."

Garrison's face was expressionless, revealing nothing of the surge of excitement he felt. He grabbed his coat, shrugged into it without asking permission, and preceded Cullen and Dandy out of the door.

~ 4 ~

Cullen brought the shovel from the barn and shoved it into Garrison's hands. "You better dig good," Cullen said.

They had to circle around to one side of the soddy in order to find a way to climb up to the rise behind it. The snow was hip deep most of the way and the going was heavy. Cullen led the way, plowing a deep furrow, and Garrison followed. Dandy lagged behind, keeping his distance.

Garrison saw that Dandy carried a rifle, and that he wore gloves.

Cullen and Garrison struggled to the top of the slope into which the soddy had been set. Dandy stopped halfway up the rise, apparently not relishing the labored climb through deep drifts. He came only far enough to see over the edge of the sloping roof. From this vantage he had a clear view of the area where Garrison was to dig.

Cautiously Cullen took up a position well clear of the roof itself. He stood looking down from the rise, his back to the wind, in the darkness like a massive rock set on the hill.

Disappointed, Garrison began to dig. He had hoped to get Dandy closer, or to have the two men bunched together. If no other possibility presented itself, he believed he could outrun Cullen, aided by the darkness and the spitting snow. But Dandy was the dangerous one.

Still, standing at the side where he was, the little gunman could not be sure of seeing everything that Garrison was doing. . . .

Along the slope of the roof the snow was not as deep as it was at the side of the building, measuring no more than a foot or so. It added up to a considerable weight, however. Garrison wondered just how much the roof could hold without collapsing. His maneuver to keep Cullen off the roof had been no more than a sudden hunch, which Staggs had found plausible.

Garrison began to dig at the edge of the rise where the beams of the roof butted against the hillside. Here the snow had drifted, piling up, and Garrison had two or three feet of the powdery stuff to clear away.

He shoveled the snow off to the side or threw it up on the slope above him, working as slowly as he dared. He tested the snow to see how far he could throw it, and he tried to judge the effect of the wind. He was also testing the reactions of the men who watched him—Cullen above him on the hill, no more than six feet away, standing knee deep in a drift, Dandy off to the left and slightly below him.

When he dumped a shovelful of snow toward Dandy, throwing it high, the wind caught some of the white winter dust and blew it into Dandy's face. The little gunfighter cursed him. "Damn it, watch where you're throwin' that!"

But he took it, Garrison noted. Powder in his face had angered him without arousing suspicion. He was too absorbed in his particular miseries to concentrate fully on what Garrison might be up to. After all, what could an unarmed man do while two men guarded him?

Light spilled across the yard below. Staggs emerged from the soddy, walking straight out from the door far enough so that he could see above the roof line. "How

the hell long's this gonna take? Haven't you found anything yet?"

"Snow's deep," Garrison called down.

He went back to his digging. His heart was thudding
now, more with excitement than from his labors. He
could not stall much longer. He hoped Staggs would go
back inside where it was warm. He had come out without
his heavy jacket, a hopeful sign.

After a moment Garrison glanced over his shoulder.
Staggs was gone; the door had closed to shut off the wash
of light across the snow. In its aftermath the night
seemed darker.

Garrison threw a look at Dandy. The slender figure was
hunched over, shoulders pulled in tight. He felt the cold,
Garrison thought with grim satisfaction. Cullen, by contrast, seemed oblivious of any discomfort. He stood placidly, not bothering to brush the white dust from his
shoulders, watching Garrison with an interest that appeared almost friendly. If Cullen was carrying a gun, it
was buried under his heavy coat. It would take him a
long time to reach it, and even then he would either have
to drag off a glove or risk a clumsy shot. Dandy, on the
other hand, could fire his rifle without taking gloves off if
he had to.

But Dandy had his arms folded across his chest, hugging himself for warmth. The rifle was hanging from the
crook of one arm.

Good enough, Garrison thought. Dandy wasn't expecting anything. His carelessness might give Garrison an
extra second or two.

He studied the blackness of the sky. The storm was im-
penetrable. He couldn't wait in the hope of heavier snow.
Dandy would soon be getting impatient, and Staggs
might reappear at any moment. He hadn't worn a coat
when he came out, but he had carried his own gun in its

holster at his hip and Garrison's six-shooter in his waist-band.

Garrison dug deep into the snow, filling his shovel with as much as it would carry. Then he bent forward, peering at the sod revealed beneath the snow. The movement took him partially out of Dandy's view. Cullen's curiosity was awakened and the big man took a step forward.

Garrison lifted his shovel in one swift motion, hefting a great pile of snow, and threw it directly at Dandy. Garrison let the shovel swing high, brought his left hand down the handle to meet his right, and swung the blade of the shovel in a full arc toward Cullen's legs.

He heard Dandy's angry shout but there was no time to look at him. It was Cullen who surprised him. The big man nimbly evaded the vicious swing of the shovel and lunged forward.

Garrison dodged away to his right, avoiding Cullen and also moving away from Dandy, trying to get Cullen between them to block off any shot by the gunman. The big man leaped after Garrison.

Then it happened. Cullen's rush carried him onto the slanting sod roof. When he jumped to intercept Garrison his full weight came down. His boot shot straight through the roof, through snow and sod and layered poles. He dropped to one knee with a bellow of surprise and pain, and there he was stuck, caught like a bear in a trap, his leg jutting through the roof into the room below.

Garrison did not wait to see more. He dropped the shovel and ran—at least as much of a run as he could manage through the uneven drifts. He went up the slope to the crest of the hill where the snow was thinner, blown off by the wind to settle into creases and hollows lower down. Then he raced to his right, angling away from the house.

Instinct made him veer off after a dozen yards. He

heard the whack of Dandy's rifle, heard—or imagined—
the *zinggg!* of a bullet passing close to his ear.

He had gained ground in the first moments of surprise.
Now the darkness and the wind, gusting suddenly to
throw up a whirling cloud of snow, came to his aid.
Dandy had to get closer to be sure of hitting him, and
Garrison meant to make the pursuit as punishing as possi-
ble.

He struck off for the high ground north of the soddy,
where the land climbed all the way to the rim overlooking the canyon. Dandy would have to follow him through
the deep snow he didn't like. Garrison bulled his way
through the more shallow drifts, slipping and stumbling
over uneven terrain whose treacherous dips and breaks
were hidden. Where the snow piled too high and was not
packed enough to clamber over, he had to change his
course, first trying one, then another passage until he
fought his way through to firmer ground. Within minutes
he was laboring, each cold breath like a knife striking
deep into his lungs.

He risked a glance over his shoulder. His ragged tracks
carved a small canyon through the snow, twisting this
way and that, extending back down the slope toward the
soddy, vanishing into darkness. Dandy was not visible.

Garrison plunged on. The next time he looked back he
saw a splash of light that marked the front of the soddy,
whose shape could no longer be seen. Staggs had joined
the hunt.

And closer—much closer—there was a blur of movement along Garrison's trail. Dandy was chasing him, following in his tracks where the going was made easier.

There was little cover on the long climb except for that
provided by the uneven drifts and the darkness. Little
snow was falling now. There was only the powder
whipped up and blown about by the wind.

He wondered why there had been no more shots, at least none that he had heard. Staggs might still want him alive, but he doubted that Dandy would hold his fire now. The gunman probably wanted to get closer, making sure of his target this time.

Staggs' presence ruled out any chance that Garrison might have been able to circle to his right and head downslope, gaining speed and distance. He could only continue to climb in the feeble hope that his pursuers would wear out sooner than he came to the end of his rope. His legs were dead weights now, his chest heaving, each breath a raw and painful gasp.

Then he heard the crack of a rifle once more. The sound came to him thin, brittle, muffled by the wind and the blowing snow. Could Dandy see him clearly? Or Staggs?

Garrison looked back. Halfway down the slope, Dandy lifted his rifle to his shoulder for another shot.

Garrison threw himself into a snowbank. As soon as he heard the shot he scrambled up and ran.

Underestimated him, Garrison thought numbly as he plodded on, slower now, driving himself by force of will, ignoring the pain and the cold and the desire to rest weary legs. Dandy was gaining. Taking advantage of the tunnel Garrison had carved in his blundering flight, the gunman was closing the gap. All that complaining and those fancy clothes were deceptive. He seemed like a man who would give up easily, not liking the feel of snow in his boots or a knife in his lungs. But he was still coming. Maybe the killing urge did it, Garrison thought. Maybe that was all Dandy needed to keep him coming.

Garrison reached some kind of a shelf. Suddenly his way was clearer. The ground was more level here, and because it was a high table exposed to the full lash of the wind the snow cover was thin. He forced his aching legs into another desperate run.

He saw the black well of the canyon just in time.

Garrison pulled up at the very rim of the steep-walled ravine, heart jumping. He swung around. As if a curtain had lifted for a moment, the air was clear of blowing snow. Through the darkness he saw the vague shape that must be Staggs far below him to his left.

Then Dandy stepped around a shoulder not thirty yards away.

For a moment the two men faced each other across the white expanse. Garrison thought he heard Staggs shout "No!" The cry was lost in the slam of Dandy's rifle.

Turning away as he heard the shot, Garrison felt the blow of the bullet like a kick in the back. It picked him up and blew him off his feet. And the rim was there, too close. He fell into the yawning blackness of the canyon, trailed by a startled yell.

The yell cut off abruptly, and there was no sound but the blowing wind.

CHAPTER 5

～ 1 ～

A shadow moved near the barn. The shadow had been there for some time, unnoticed except for one brief glimpse by Garrison. When he had looked at it directly, trying to confirm a fleeting impression of movement, the shadow had vanished.

Now it paused, dark eyes studying the house. The two men with guns had returned to the house, both angry, the blockier man berating the other one. A third man had had to be helped down from the roof of the house. He was huge, and when one of the men supporting him had slipped and the giant also fell, he had let out a bellow of pain. The others had had a hard time lifting him again to carry him into the soddy.

The dark eyes watching the house were thoughtful. Finally, satisfied that the men inside would not emerge again soon, the shadow slipped silently away from the barn, moving past the corral and down a gentle slope to the bed of the creek, which was frozen over except where someone had broken through the ice. Coming to the bank, the shadow turned left, following the meandering path of the stream toward the canyon.

At the mouth of the draw the shadow paused again. The dark eyes peered back at the house, then looked ahead. The snow was formidably deep at the bottom of the canyon, a wall of snow nearly ten feet high. There was a trickle of water at the base of this snow mass where the creek made its own tunnel.

The shadow hesitated before this barrier of snow. The man who had been shot had fallen from the top of the bluff into the canyon. He was almost certainly dead. If still alive, wounded and helpless, he would not survive the night.

The shadow stiffened. From somewhere up the canyon a sound cracked the icy stillness of the night. A snuffling, scrabbling sound. The shadow felt hairs rise at the back of his neck.

Another creature was moving along the canyon.

The presence of this newcomer banished the shadowy figure's doubts. He moved closer to the uneven west wall of the ravine, searching for handholds and footings. Slowly he began to work his way into the dark cut, fighting the snow.

Ahead of him the snuffling sound became a growl.

2

Garrison lay motionless. His mind, swimming to consciousness, focused on the pain in his side. After a moment he explored the wound with numb fingers. The snow and cold had stanched the bleeding. He wondered how long he had been lying there, and why neither Staggs nor Dandy had come to finish him off.

In the darkness Dandy's aim had been slightly off target. The bullet had grazed Garrison's rib cage, missing his heart by about four inches.

He lay in a deep cup of snow carved by the impact of his body when he fell from the rim high above. The snow all around him was several feet above his head, but he was only half buried.

He heard the soft pad of movement, very close by. A new chill touched the back of his neck.

When Garrison stirred, trying to sit up, the pain in his side brought an unwanted gasp. Moreover, the weight of the snow covering the lower half of his body pinned him. The snow beneath him, by contrast, seemed to have no body at all. Any movement caused his torso to sink deeper into the softness.

It was black there at the bottom of the canyon, but not so dark that he failed to see the glitter of two eyes peering down at him over the edge of the snow cup. Garrison stared back.

He struggled briefly against the white prison in which he lay, but each effort only caused him to sink deeper, as if into quicksand.

The wolf crouched at the edge of the pit gave a low growl.

Unable to move, Garrison watched the lean, gaunt animal prowl along the soft edge of the pit, treading so lightly that he did not sink very deep, yet clearly worried about the softness of the snow.

He had to be starving, Garrison thought with a curious detachment. Otherwise he would never take the chance.

A small section of the snowbank crumbled. Snow sifted over Garrison in a soft, silent avalanche. More of the middle of his body was now covered, leaving only his head and shoulders and his right arm free.

The wolf appeared at another portion of the pit's rim, snarling again—more in frustration, Garrison suspected, than for any other reason. The wolf was afraid to be buried in an avalanche of his own making, but he was not ready to give up so easy a prey.

Garrison dragged his left arm free, but even so small a movement brought more snow down around his head.

He watched the wolf ease forward. Lying flat, hugging

the snow, the wolf began to wriggle over the edge of the bank. His head and shoulders came fully into view. His front legs worked over the edge.

Suddenly the snow gave way. Garrison heard a snarling yelp. Then a white wall buried him.

 3

"You hear something?" Staggs was on his feet.

"What's there to hear?" Dandy's tone was surly with resentment. Staggs had climbed all over him for shooting Garrison, claiming the man was trapped and couldn't get away.

"Sounded like a shot."

"Well, there ain't nobody out there doin' any shootin' now. Garrison didn't have no gun on him."

Staggs went to the door and opened it. For a moment he stood in the doorway, staring toward the canyon to the north, his head cocked, listening. Bitter cold blew in through the open door. Staggs closed it slowly. "Maybe he ain't dead," he muttered, turning back into the room. "We don't know that for sure."

"I hit him," Dandy said. "I don't miss anybody that close. And it must be a hundred-foot drop into that canyon where he went down. If he's alive, he won't be doin' any more running."

"We oughta make sure."

"Then you do it," Dandy said. "You don't like the way me and Cullen handled things, you can do it yourself. There's enough snow in that bottom so you couldn't even see the top of Cullen's hat if he was standin' in it. I ain't goin' in there, not anyways while it's dark."

Staggs leveled a stare at him. "You're the one put him

there. Come morning, you'll damned well make sure he's finished."

Dandy was silent. There were times when he was only a hair away from facing up to Staggs and calling him. This wasn't one of those times. That uphill push in Garrison's tracks had damned near finished *him*. If Garrison hadn't come up against the edge of the bluff when he did, if he had kept going another minute he would have been all alone out there. Dandy was convinced that he could not have followed Garrison another twenty yards without falling on his face.

A groan from Cullen diverted Dandy's dark thoughts of Garrison. Dandy looked at the big man, who lay on the floor near the fire, his eyes half closed and dull with pain. Dandy was tired, frustrated and angry, but Cullen was a lot worse off.

When Cullen broke through the roof he tore up his left leg. At first it had appeared that the leg was broken. Staggs and Dandy had had to open up the hole in the roof to free the leg. When Cullen tried to step on that foot he bellowed in pain and collapsed. Cullen falling like that was like the biggest tree in the forest coming down. The whole woods shook.

With great difficulty they had managed to get the big man down off the roof and into the house. There a closer examination had indicated that there were no bones broken. The broken poles of the roof had lacerated Cullen's calf in a messy way and torn up something in his ankle. Staggs had forced the woman to clean and bandage the leg. Then Staggs had slit Cullen's boot and stuffed his bandaged foot back into it, before the ankle became too swollen to fit inside the slit boot. Cullen was then able to hobble around a little, using the long-handled shovel as a crude crutch with the blade shoved up under his armpit.

Brooding, Dandy said, "You still think that money is buried up on the roof?"

Staggs glowered at him. They would dig up the whole roof if need be when it was light, but no one really believed the money was there.

"I think Garrison fooled us," Dandy said. "Maybe the money ain't here at all."

"It's here!" Staggs snarled. "It's got to be! And if we don't find it, we'll just sit here until Virgil comes home. Sooner or later, he'll come for it."

Dandy said nothing to this. In fact, the idea of waiting for Pryor made him uneasy. There were few men who could put the fear in him. He was not even afraid of Staggs in the way Virgil Pryor made him nervous and unsure of himself. He had been present once when Pryor drew on a young, big-talking gunslick. Pryor had put three bullets into the kid before he could clear the leather. Dandy had never seen anything else that fast, or that deadly.

"*She* knows." Dandy nodded significantly toward the sleeping alcove.

"Maybe. I'm not so sure."

"I say if we don't find that money in the mornin', leave me alone with her. I'll find out what she knows."

Staggs considered this in silence. He stared thoughtfully at the woman. He did not think she was asleep, although she lay with her back to the room, huddled under her blankets.

He thought about the way she had acted when she heard that Garrison had gone over. No screaming, no caterwauling. It wasn't natural, not if there were anything between her and Garrison the way Staggs had had it figured. She just stared at Dandy when he blurted it out, as if he had come in from outside to announce that it was snowing, her eyes as dry as dust. It wasn't natural.

Unless she was Virgil Pryor's woman all the way, after all. Which made Garrison mean nothing to her, merely a man Virgil had left there to look after things. Or, as Garrison had claimed himself, someone who had drifted by.

Staggs had had trouble all along fitting Garrison into this situation. He was not the kind of hardcase you would expect Virgil Pryor to hire. Maybe that was the whole problem about understanding Garrison. It could be that he was nothing but a no-account drifter.

And that led Staggs to only one conclusion: The woman alone could possess knowledge of where Pryor had buried the money he stole from his partners.

Staggs' lips curled in his semblance of a grin. Behind it this time, however, there was a cruel amusement. He was thinking of Dandy's way with a woman. Dressed in his fancy clothes and with his handsome face, Dandy could always get a woman to go up the stairs with him once. Few, if any, would have him a second time. Not willingly.

"All right," Staggs said. "First light we make sure Garrison's done for. Then, if we don't find that money on the roof where Garrison said it was, you get to reason with her. All the time you want."

Pryor's woman was hidden by her blankets, but Staggs was certain that he saw her body stiffen.

~ 4 ~

It couldn't be hell, Garrison thought. Hell wasn't supposed to be this cold.

He tried to sit up too quickly, wincing as pain grabbed his side. Touching the area of the wound, he was surprised to discover that it was tightly bound in strips of cloth, apparently torn from an old but clean shirt.

He had no idea where he was or how he had gotten there. He was inside some kind of shack or shed, small and dark. There was only a dirt floor. Through cracks in the planks that formed the wall Garrison was able to perceive grayness, a shade lighter than the interior of the shack.

Something moved and Garrison's hand went to his holster. Empty, of course. Everything came back to him in a rush then: his fall from the bluff, his helpless struggles while the wolf prowled above him, and the cave-in. . . .

A man chuckled softly. "You would shoot me if you had a gun, *señor?* Maybe I should have left you to the wolf, eh?"

Garrison made out the shape of the man, the white shine of his teeth as he smiled. A small, wiry man, wearing a wide-brimmed Mexican sombrero. "People been trying to put me under," Garrison drawled. "Thought maybe you was one of 'em." He paused. "Name's Garrison. Who might you be? Wait a minute. *¿Como te llamas?* Ramon?"

There was a brief silence. Then the wiry man said, "Sí. Ramon Sanudo. But how do you know this, *señor?*"

"She told me."

"Mrs. Pryor?" Sanudo's surprise was plain in his voice. "She told you of me?"

"That's right. She spoke of two men who worked for Pryor: you and Pegleg Parks. I met Parks in town."

"I do not understand. Who are these men who tried to kill you? Why is Parks not here? And what of *la señora?* What has been done to her?"

Garrison described what Trish Lovell had told him about Parks breaking his leg and having to be taken into town. Then he told of his own coming to the ranch, and of the unexpected arrival of the three outlaws, catching him by surprise. "Pryor and these others robbed a bank.

Leastwise, that's what they say, and I have no reason to believe otherwise."

"Why are they here? *Señor* Pryor is not with them."

"They say Pryor cheated them out of the stolen money. They were partners, and Pryor double-crossed them. They think the money is buried here somewhere—that Pryor brought it back with him when he lit out." Garrison paused. He was beginning to be able to make out Ramon Sanudo's face in the dimness of the shack, but he could not see clearly enough to read any reaction to his account. "Is it possible the money's here somewhere?"

Sanudo's shoulders lifted in a barely perceptible shrug. "Anything is possible."

"You believe Pryor could've robbed a bank like they say?"

"*Sí, es posible.* He is a bad man."

Garrison's tone was dry. "If you know that, why do you work for him?"

Ramon Sanudo smiled. "If I would work only for a good man, and if I would always know that he is a good man, I would have very empty pockets, I think."

Grudgingly Garrison nodded. A man couldn't always pick a soft place to fall. He had worked for good and bad himself. A man who was always drifting on, as he had done, accepted what he found along the way and made the best of it. Ramon Sanudo was no different.

If you wanted to shape things your own way, Garrison thought, you would have to light somewhere. You would have to build something of your own. This thought was a new one for him, and he examined it for a moment, wondering what had put it into his head.

"What happened to that wolf?" he asked after a moment. "Did you shoot him?"

"It was dark. I think I missed him. But he was not so hungry when he smelled the powder, I think."

Garrison considered what must have happened in the canyon. A gunshot and a tumble in the snow had scared off the wolf. Had that shot also been heard by others?

"If they heard the shot, that means they could know someone else is around besides me." He looked around the tiny shack. It was a crude shelter, the boards of the walls warped and revealing wide cracks through which the cold seeped. "Where are we?"

"It is nothing now—an empty shack. Once there were tools kept here . . . like this." He lifted a branding iron so that Garrison could see it. Garrison wondered if the Mexican had been holding the iron as a weapon if needed. Peering at the brand, Garrison made out the crude initials MB. Not Virgil Pryor's brand.

"You know those partners of Pryor's are trouble. Are they likely to find this place easily? How far are we from the house?"

"Five . . . maybe six kilometers."

"That's about three miles, isn't it?"

Ramon shrugged off the question. "It is far enough, and they would not know of this crib. It is not so easy to see if you do not know where it is."

Garrison eased cautiously into a sitting position, his back against the wall. "We're still on Pryor's place, I take it."

"*Sí.*"

"You worked here a long time? For Pryor?"

"It was not always *Señor* Pryor's place. Once it was the ranch of *Señor* Burden. He was a good man. I worked for him many years. We hunted the longhorn cattle in the brush country, very hard work—but good." Sanudo was silent for a moment. "Two years ago I went to visit my family. When I returned, *Señor* Pryor was here."

"What happened to Burden?"

"*Señor* Pryor said that he bought the place and Burden

moved on." The words were noncommittal, but Garrison caught the skepticism behind them. Then Sanudo added, "*Señor* Burden had worked very hard. It was many years before there were enough cattle to be sold. He built the house with his own hands. . . ."

"You don't think he sold out." It was a statement, not a question.

"*Señor* Pryor said that it was so. No one questions such a man."

"All the more reason for you to pick up stakes," Garrison suggested speculatively. "You liked Burden, but you go on punching cows for Pryor."

Ramon Sanudo smiled once more. "I am like the wolf. When he is hungry, he will do many things he doesn't want to do. He will even eat you, *Señor* Garrison."

Garrison laughed. "Thanks to you, he didn't." He glanced through the cracks in the wall. There was a faint lightening in the grayness outside. There were trees nearby, sheltering the shack. It would be daybreak soon; he had been out most of the night. "How'd you get me here?"

"I did not carry you far, *señor*. But my horse did."

"They'll be able to track us here, soon as it's light enough for them to see by."

"I do not think there are any tracks. There has been too much wind, and more snow. It has been many hours, *Señor* Garrison. You can look outside. Even I could not find my own tracks." Sanudo went to the door, which hung on one leather hinge, and scraped it open to peer out, as if to verify his claim about the tracks. "I think you will be safe here. They have your horse, *señor*?"

"In the barn." He scowled as he guessed what was in Sanudo's mind. "Where are you going, Ramon?"

"The *señora* is alone now. I cannot leave her alone with such men. She is not one like *Señor* Pryor."

"You don't have a chance dealing a lone hand," Garrison said bluntly.

"It must be done," the Mexican said simply. "I have only one horse, *Señor* Garrison. I cannot ask her to carry two men through so much snow where I must ride. And I do not think you are ready to walk far. You are lucky you are not a dead man."

"They'll be lookin' for me to make sure. When they find I'm not in that canyon, they'll start hunting. They'll find some sign if they look hard enough."

"Maybe they will leave the *señora* alone in the house," Ramon suggested hopefully. "Then I will take her away. What else is there for me to do? Do you wish to leave her with those *bandidos?*"

Garrison felt a growing respect for the Mexican hand. Garrison tried to struggle to his feet, teeth set against the pain in his side. He was not prepared for the sudden dizziness, the weakness in his legs, the general aches that pervaded his whole body, battered by his long fall into the canyon. Even soft snow made a punishing mattress at the end of such a drop. "You'll need someone to back you up," he said.

"You would only slow me down," Sanudo said gently. "I must move quickly."

"Damn it, those men are just as bad as Pryor—just as dangerous. They'll make mincemeat of you!"

"First they must find me," Ramon Sanudo said. "If I do not come back, *Señor* Garrison, you will find my rifle in the corner there. She is old, but she shoots straight. That is all I can do."

He smiled, tugged the door open, and was gone.

CHAPTER 6

～ 1 ～

Sometimes with the passing of a winter storm the new day could take your breath away, offering a sky that was a limitless, sparkling blue over the dazzling-white landscape, with a gentle breeze, the air crisp and clean and intoxicating as good wine. For someone like Ramon Sanudo, who had lived all of his life more or less in the open, close to the land with all its blessings and indifferent cruelties, such mornings were like the prayers of his childhood. They spoke of God and all of the goodness of life.

This morning, however, he gazed upon the clear sky at dawn with misgivings. A dark, blustery day would have been more to his liking. Continued snow would have been this day's blessing.

From a mile off, concealed by a small grove of brush oak, he could see the Pryor soddy and the nearby barn clearly in the distance. His eyes were still keen, and he was able to observe two tiny figures emerge from the house and move off toward the canyon north of the ranch buildings.

But this meant that he too could be easily seen over great distances in the open. He would have to circle to the southwest and approach the soddy from behind, using all the cover he could find. This land, of course, was as familiar to him as the scratchings of his own palm. He knew every crevice, every rise or fall of the terrain, every tree. But such a cautious, circuitous approach would take time.

The two men who had left the house obviously intended to search the canyon for Garrison's body. When they did not find it quickly, how long would they remain in the canyon? How much time did Ramon have?

And where was the third outlaw? Garrison had spoken of three men only, and Ramon had observed all three when he had furtively approached the house the previous afternoon—made wary by the presence of strangers and alarmed by the discovery of another man tied to a post at the corner of the barn. One of the three badmen Ramon had seen was a giant. From a mile off he could not be certain, but he believed the other two had set off on foot for the canyon.

The third must be in the house. The giant.

He presented a formidable obstacle, but would a better chance present itself? Ramon Sanudo was an expert with a gun or a knife. Against one man, particularly if he had the advantage of surprise, he might succeed in rescuing the *señora*, whom he liked and respected. Against three . . . He shrugged fatalistically.

It had occurred to him that he might simply turn away and ride south, abandoning the woman to her fate. But the thought was only a passing one. While he did not much care for *Señor* Pryor, the *señora* was not the same. And if he did not seek to protect her, who would? Not Garrison, who had apparently tried. Of no use now was a battered, wounded man who could not even sit up without setting his jaws tightly against the pain. Pryor, if he were there, might well be the equal of three men—but he had been absent for months. Only Ramon Sanudo could help the *señora* now. Clearly, it was his duty.

He had also given thought to the stolen money Garrison had told him about. He wondered if the story was true. A man might easily begin to dream about finding such a bounty, and Ramon Sanudo was not immune to the lure of buried treasure. But he was also a realist, and the prospect of stealing from Virgil Pryor, knowing that Pryor would pursue him relentlessly, sent a chill chasing along his spine, like footsteps over his grave.

When the two slow-moving figures had disappeared finally into the mouth of the canyon, Sanudo began his cautious approach. He rode south and then cut across a bench that was shielded from the area of the house by some low bunchgrass hills. The route he chose provided concealment and also enabled him to avoid deep drifts. He made good time.

Ten minutes later he concealed his horse in a sheltered ravine southwest of the soddy. He covered the last hundred meters on foot. He approached the soddy itself from behind, so that when he crawled over the last rise he was looking down at its roof.

He peered off toward the canyon mouth, now almost directly north of him. The glare of morning sunlight off the new-fallen snow was so bright that he had to shield his eyes with his hands and squint.

He saw no one. The two searchers had had time to discover that Garrison was missing. Perplexed, they would have been compelled to continue the search. How could a dead man disappear? If they had thought him alive they would surely have gone into the canyon after him last night. The deep snow at the bottom of the draw would make their search difficult, delaying them. But for how long?

Soon, he reasoned, they would turn back. It was also possible, in spite of what Ramon had told Garrison, that the light fall of snow during the night had not completely covered his trail. If they found this sign, and read it correctly, they would give up their fruitless exploration of the canyon and seek to follow his tracks.

If Ramon Sanudo was to have any chance of rescuing the *señora* with the golden hair, surely it was now, before the other outlaws returned. The possibility excited him. The man below him in the house, the giant, expected nothing. He might be lazy, inattentive, even asleep.

Ramon studied an alteration in the roof's contours thoughtfully. A hole had been made in the roof. By appearances, this had happened recently. During Garrison's escape? It must be so. Ramon had not been close enough to see what was happening in the darkness. A buffalo hide had been laid over the opening in the roof, its edges weighed down with a few stones, broken sod and loose dirt, in a hasty attempt to seal off the hole against snow and cold. Some light snow had partially covered the repair during the night.

Was the hole large enough to admit a man? Ramon Sanudo was a short man, but he was no longer slender. Ah, if he would always eat the tortillas and frijoles prepared by Marta, as he had recently, he would not fit into his clothes, much less through the narrow opening in the roof of the soddy.

He considered the possibility. It would be an awkward entrance even if he could manage to squeeze through the hole, and during the act of passage he would be vulnerable. Even the idea of pulling the hide quickly from the opening so that he could shoot into the room below did not please him. The giant might be in the wrong part of the room, and then he would be forewarned.

No. He must be caught by surprise.

Ramon Sanudo made his decision. There was no longer any time to waste in speculation and indecision. The others would return all too soon. He must do what he had to do before they turned back. All he needed was a good throw with his knife. There would be no sound. . . .

He slid back and to the side, careful not to set any weight on the slanting section of built-up roof. The snow muffled his movements as he crept around to the side of the house where the rise dropped away. He began his descent.

Halfway down he froze.

He lay absolutely motionless. Another yard or two and he would be behind the house, invisible from its north side, but he dared not crawl another foot.

The two badmen had just emerged from the canyon.

Could they have seen him? He did not know. They had not visibly reacted, but that might be a ruse.

He was partially hidden by the snow, but he could not be certain how well he was concealed. If the men looked directly at him, surely they would detect something. Not his sombrero. Fortunately he had had the sense to leave it behind, with his horse. It was a fine sombrero from Chihuahua with a wide brim and a tall crown. He had not wanted to risk losing it, and it was this fear, rather than the thought of concealment, that had made him take it off. So there was no hat for the badmen to detect, but they might see something else. A depression in the snow that had not been there before. A portion of his body protruding . . .

Cautiously he wormed deeper into the snow. At the same time he edged toward the deeper drifts at the side of the house.

He lifted his eye to the edge of the snowbank.

His heart thumped. The two men were well away from the canyon, crossing the open shelf below the stream. They were not coming toward the soddy but moving slowly eastward. And they were studying something along the ground as they walked.

His tracks, Ramon thought. Perhaps he should not have spoken so confidently to *Señor* Garrison.

Suddenly the two men changed direction, veering toward the barn. When they drew close to it they stopped to talk briefly. Ramon Sanudo took this opportunity to crawl hastily to lower ground, disappearing completely into the deep snow. Now they could not see him—but that did not mean they would fail to notice a fresh disturbance in the snow if they returned to the house.

He heard their voices. One called out sharply. "Tell him to stay awake!"

"Yeah, yeah." The second man was closer. He sounded surly, out of sorts. Perhaps he had not relished this morning's burrowing through the canyon drifts.

Ramon lay tense, heart pounding. The time of danger was now, as one of the men approached the house. Ramon could not hear anything, and he dared not lift his head for another look.

Then there was the sound of the door opening, a familiar creaking from one of the hinges. A murmur of voices, the words not clear. The deep rumble of one man's reply: That must be the giant in the house.

A moment later the other man's voice came clearly. "Just stay put and keep your eye on her. Ain't no way that sumbitch is gonna try comin' back here, hurt like he is, but watch out anyways. We'll find him. He can't have got far, and if he's still alive we'll bring him back so's you can stomp him with your good leg." The man laughed at his own humor.

Ramon heard the sound of the door closing and, faintly, the crunch of footsteps fading across the snow toward the barn.

Stomp him with your good leg. Ramon Sanudo considered the meaning of this remark. Was the giant injured? How badly? It must have happened during the fighting;

otherwise Garrison would have said something about the big man being crippled. Garrison had said only that all three were badmen, worthy partners for Virgil Pryor.

It was hard waiting in his well of snow, unable to see anything but snow glittering like white gold in the sunlight just inches from his eyes. But Ramon Sanudo was a patient man, and he did not move for several minutes. During that time he heard the blowing of a horse brought from the barn into the cold, the whinny of another, the jingling of metal and rubbing of leather as the horses were saddled. The two men were obviously riding off. They would not try to follow his tracks very far on foot.

At last Ramon lifted his head to peer over the snowbank. At that instant one of the men on horseback glanced over his shoulder toward the house.

Ramon ducked back into his hole. *¡Madre de Dios!* Had he been seen? He felt the wild thudding of his heart as he lay on his chest in the snow, listening intently. It seemed impossible that he had not been spotted.

Silence.

When his curiosity could no longer be contained, Ramon lifted an eye slowly into the open.

White teeth flashed in a broad grin. The two outlaws were far along the shelf above the creek, following the trail Ramon had taken the night before when he carried Garrison away. They were finding the tracking slow, for the wind and fresh snowfall during the night had wiped out or obscured most of the sign Ramon had left behind. They kept losing the trail, frequently stopping to cast around until they picked it up again.

At this pace it would take them a long time to find their way to the shack where Ramon Sanudo had left Garrison. The shack was on a higher bench, invisible from below, which was why he had chosen it as a refuge

for the night. The two trackers would not know where
the trail was leading them until it looped around a fall of
rocks and climbed suddenly.

By then, if he was fortunate, *Señor* Garrison would be
aware of them.

Ramon Sanudo considered Garrison's danger for a moment, but there was nothing Ramon could do. The fate of
the *señora* was of even greater urgency. She was a prisoner of these outlaws in part because he, Ramon Sanudo,
had left her alone. It was true that he could not have
known that Pegleg Parks would break his good leg, but it
had happened nevertheless. And Patricia Pryor had been
left to the doubtful mercy of unscrupulous men.

Ramon continued to wait for some minutes after the
retreating forms of the two men on horseback had disappeared far down the shelf, hidden finally behind a wind-
carved crest of snow that resembled a giant wave frozen
at the moment it was about to break. At last he rose and
eased his way silently to the corner of the soddy.

The big man inside had had time to relax his vigilance.
In spite of his partner's cautionary warning, the giant
would expect no one. Certainly not so soon after his partners had left . . .

Ramon listened for any sound of voices within the
house. He had heard enough in the outlaws' brief conversation to verify that the *señora* was there, a prisoner, but
he could detect no sound of activity. There was only a
brooding silence that matched the great silence of the
snow-covered world outside.

A gunshot would be heard far off on this bright, clear
morning, and the two outlaws following his trail were not
far enough away to be out of earshot. Should he wait?
No. There was another way.

Ramon Sanudo slid his long knife from its scabbard.

The soddy was small, and he could spear a leaf at ten paces with his knife.

Surprise now was everything. He must strike before the big man could recover enough to get off a betraying shot.

Ramon crept along the front wall of the soddy, making no sound at all on the cushion of snow. He dropped low to pass under the single front window.

Then he was at the door, pausing once more to listen.

Trish Lovell said, "Do you want more coffee?"

"I'd like that fine," Cullen said. "It's mighty good coffee, ma'am."

Ramon tried to place the voices exactly. The woman had spoken from the side of the room to his left, the area of the hearth. The big man was to the right of the door.

Good, Ramon thought. The door, as he faced it, swung on hinges at its left side. He would have an immediate view of the interior to his right as the door opened. And the *señora* was safely out of the way.

He reached for the latch. His free hand gripped the knife, holding it lightly as one might hold a bird in the hand.

He saw it all in his mind before he made his move—the quick release of the latch, the thrust of his shoulder against the door, and the simultaneous leap into the opening, his right hand already flashing forward to throw the knife. It happened exactly as he had planned it, except that the big man was waiting for him.

~ 2 ~

Cullen's brain worked slowly but with a dogged single-mindedness. Dandy had told him to remain alert and to watch the woman. Garrison was missing, which meant that he was still alive. He might attempt to return to the house while Dandy and Staggs were gone. Cullen was alert.

As he waited, Cullen's perception of his vigil underwent an odd change. It seemed to him that he was not so much obliged to make sure Pryor's woman did not escape as to protect her.

He liked her. She was quiet and she was pretty. Cullen had never been alone with a woman as pretty as this one, and when she spoke to him he found himself uneasy, his tongue thick. Yet he could hardly take his eyes from her.

He did so, however, when a shadow fell across the bottom of the door.

The house faced east. The doorway was directly in line with the rays of the morning sun. The door fit well enough, but there remained a gap at the bottom, hardly more than a quarter of an inch, making a narrow bar of light. When a shadow broke that bar of light Cullen knew without thinking that someone was outside.

He lurched to his feet, holding the shovel he used as a crutch. His coat hung on a peg near the door. His gun was stuffed into one of the pockets. A rifle was also there, leaning against the wall. Neither were within Cullen's reach as the door burst open.

Cullen felt surprise at sight of a wiry man he had never seen before. It was not Garrison! He saw the man's upraised arm and the glitter of sunlight on a steel blade. Knowledge of danger and a reflexive rage were instantaneous. The knife flashed forward. Cullen heard the woman's stifled scream.

The big man bellowed in pain as the blade struck deep into his belly. He staggered forward. Suddenly his big hands slid down the long handle of the shovel to grip the end of the handle. He swung the shovel, blade out, in a sweeping, powerful blow. It struck the open door, but the strength of the blow was such that the point of the shovel bit through a half inch of wood and continued onward with scarcely any loss of force. The edge of steel caught the wiry Mexican before he could jump clear. It sliced across his body just under the rib cage, opening up his belly as cleanly as a knife gutting an antelope.

There was a roaring in Cullen's head. He thought he could also hear distant screams, those of Trish Lovell and of the Mexican. The Mexican staggered backward over the snow piled in front of the house. One hand at his middle tried to hold his split belly together while the other hand dug for the six-gun in his holster. Cullen stalked him. His wrecked ankle wobbled and he almost fell. His legs were strangely heavy as he dragged himself forward. The Mexican retreated from him. The two men moved very slowly, as if they walked in a river, a river red with their blood.

Cullen had almost reached the Mexican when his six-gun roared. The impact of the bullet stopped Cullen in his tracks, stopped him where the knife still buried in his flesh had not.

The Mexican sank to his knees. He could no longer hold his torn body intact and the six-gun was suddenly too heavy to lift. He fell forward on his face. The gun discharged harmlessly.

Cullen took another step, came down on his weakened ankle and toppled forward. He landed half across the Mexican's body, his thick arms reaching out as if in an embrace. The two men lay still, frozen in that awkward embrace, like violent lovers at the end of their last, most terrible quarrel.

CHAPTER 7

The echoing crack of gunfire brought Staggs and Dandy back to the Pryor soddy at a laboring gallop. Clods of snow from the light pack flew from their horses' hoofs. They rode up behind the cover of the barn and tumbled from their horses. Staggs motioned Dandy around one side of the barn while he circled the other side.

From a corner of the barn Staggs stared at the grim scene in front of the house. One of the bodies, lying face down, had to be Cullen. Nobody else was that big.

"What do you make of it?" Dandy called out from the far side of the barn.

"I dunno."

The door of the shack stood partly open. Was anyone else there, waiting inside? Garrison, maybe?

"Mrs. Pryor?" he yelled. "You in there?"

Silence answered him, a silence that seemed to brood in the presence of death. Uneasy about that open door to the house, Staggs signalled to Dandy with his arm, pointing toward the low rise into which the soddy nestled. After a brief delay Dandy left the cover of the barn in a low, scrambling run. He circled south of the house, trying to stay out of sight of the front door. For a moment he disappeared behind high drifts. When he came into view again he was climbing the slope behind the shack.

Dandy paused, staring at the ground cover. "There's

only one set of tracks," he called out. "Whoever he is, he come alone."

Staggs approached the house then, moving cautiously, alert for a trap. But there was nothing to fear. He found Pryor's woman in the house, alone, shivering in a corner by the fireplace. Her face was white, her eyes wide and staring. When Staggs spoke to her sharply, she did not answer. It was as if she could not hear him.

He went back outside. It took only a moment to read the tableau in front of the doorway. Cullen was dead from both knife and bullet wounds. The man pinned beneath him, a stranger, had had his belly ripped open. A shovel lay near Cullen's hand, its bloodied blade staining the snow.

Staggs circled the bodies, raging. "Who is he? Who the hell is he?"

When he re-entered the shack Trish Lovell still huddled where he had found her before. When she did not respond to his questions, Staggs slapped her across the face in his anger. Her head rocked with the force of the blows. She blinked at him. Through sudden tears she seemed to see him for the first time since his return.

"Who is he?" Staggs demanded. "Who's the Mex?"

"Ramon," she whispered.

He remembered. The Mexican hand who had lit out for the border. Or had that been a lie? Had he been lurking on the ranch all along, staying out of sight, waiting for a moment when the house seemed undefended?

The questions lashed at her. When had Ramon returned? How long had she known? Where had he been hiding? What had she done to trick Cullen, letting the Mexican reach the house unseen?

She only shook her head, giving quick spasmodic jerks of denial while she went on shivering.

Finally Staggs stalked to the door. Dandy had removed

the knife from Cullen's body, and the Mexican's gunbelt. On the latter he had also found a small leather bag with a few coins inside.

"Leave them alone," Staggs ordered. "Get after Garrison. The Mex must've carried him out of the canyon. That means he's still alive."

"I knew he was hit," Dandy said. Staggs' criticism of his failure to make sure of the drifter still rankled. "Told you he never got out of that bottom by hisself. If he wasn't hurt bad he'd have been here with the greaser."

"He could still be trouble. We gotta make sure. Forget about those tracks from last night. You can backtrack along the Mexican's trail. That's fresh sign. It'll take you to where he left Garrison."

"What about you?"

"I can't leave her here alone," Staggs answered bluntly, his tone brooking no argument. "Somebody's got to stay here. Maybe Garrison ain't as bad hurt as you think. He might try to pull the same stunt the Mex did."

"What if I find him? You want me to bring him back?"

Staggs considered this only briefly. "He don't know where the money's hid. If he does, he won't talk. Kill him. Only this time make it stick."

When Dandy had disappeared beyond the soddy, Staggs set to work dragging the two bodies around to one side of the house. There he threw a blanket over them and kicked snow on top of the blanket.

Nobody wanted to look on the face of death too long.

 2

Dave Garrison had heard the shots, thin cracks of sound that carried far over the silent winter landscape. He knew at once that Ramon Sanudo was in trouble.

He wondered what had compelled the Mexican hand to go against three armed men to save a woman who belonged to another. Loyalty was a strange, unpredictable thing. So was a man's sense of honor, the line he would draw (known only to himself) that no one could cross without challenge, the burden or the danger he would accept no matter what the cost if he felt that he could not back away from it and still live with himself. Garrison had known fearful men to face death over a fancied insult. He had seen a woman shield her child from an Indian arrow with her own body. He had watched stubborn men go down over a quarrel at cards or a rivalry sparked by a painted woman's passing glance.

This was a hard land, and life did not always bring a high price. There were places, no doubt, where a man might simply laugh at an insult, shrug off a challenge, let himself be bullied or shunted aside by someone stronger, where honor and loyalty were disposable goods, readily snickered at. The West was not such a place, and few men survived there without some adherence to a personal code.

Sanudo would have flashed his broad grin on hearing such speculations, Garrison thought. Who knows why a man does what he does? *¿Quien sabe?*

Painfully Garrison struggled to his feet. He opened the door of the line shack to peer westward in the direction of the Pryor soddy. He saw that he was on a table higher than the terrain to the west, and he doubted that his hideout could be seen from below. Still, Ramon would not have been able to avoid leaving tracks this morning, even if those of the night before had been covered over. If Ramon had run into more trouble than he could handle, which now seemed probable, those tracks would bring Staggs and the others straight back to Garrison.

It would not take them long to figure out that Ramon

Sanudo had rescued him from the canyon. Which meant that they knew he was alive.

Garrison considered his situation. Even if he wanted to, he couldn't run. He had no horse, and in any event he was in no condition to ride far or fast. Besides, there was no way he could light out now to save his own hide. He might not be as foolishly reckless or romantic as the Mexican, but he had as much or more at stake. As usual he had drifted into this situation, but there was no way he could simply drift out of it, going his own way without concern for what he was leaving behind.

A man couldn't drift along forever.

This thought, by no means original or startling in the larger scheme of things, was nevertheless a new one to set up a place in Dave Garrison's mind and sit there, forcing him to take notice of it. It was the second time some such speculation had come to him during the past twenty-four hours, seeming so reasonable that it made him wonder what he had been doing with most of his adult life, just tumbleweeding along.

Hell, he must be getting delirious. That bullet wound was making him feverish in the brain.

Garrison shook his head wryly. He'd best be thinking about staying alive today, not about what he might do tomorrow.

He checked the load in the carbine Ramon Sanudo had left with him. Sanudo had preferred his close-range weapons, knife and six-shooter. Garrison was glad to have the carbine. He was in no condition to move fast. If he was going to put up any kind of fight at all, it would have to be at the longer range offered by a rifle.

He stepped outside. His whole body was bruised, stiff and sore, and each movement tugged at his side, threatening to open up the hole anew. Ramon Sanudo had done a halfway decent job of cleaning out the wound, however, and binding it with strips torn from an old shirt. It might fester if it didn't get better attention soon, but that was not something Garrison needed to fret over now.

Holding himself stiffly, Garrison circled the shack, careless of the tracks he was making, examining his position.

The snow was an enemy now. Last night, with a little help from Ramon Sanudo, it had saved his life. Now it would not only lead the outlaws straight to him, but it would also mark any new trail he made if he tried to leave the shack.

Unless he doubled along the Mexican's tracks.

With fresh interest Garrison studied the route Sanudo had taken that morning. It did not lead downward toward the lower shelf along which wound the creek. Instead it struck off toward low hills to the southwest, passing almost immediately through a stand of cedar. The trees stood black and bare against the snow, a tangle of naked trunks and branches that offered little cover.

Sanudo's route, he thought, offered a better chance to stay alive than remaining in the wooden shack. It was not sturdy enough to keep out the rain of bullets Staggs and his crew might choose to throw at him. They wouldn't even have to call him out. They could shoot right through the walls.

He sighted along the bench below him as far as he could see. There was no sign—at least none visible at a distance—of the trail Sanudo had cut last night. Suppose Staggs and the others lost that lower trail, or failed even to find it? They would not need it if the gunfire Garrison had heard meant what he believed. They could follow sign less than an hour old. There had been no snow since this morning's sunrise, and little wind. Ramon's trail would be plain, easy to follow.

For Garrison to set off in those same fresh tracks was a

clear gamble. He might blunder into the outlaws along the way.

He shrugged, the decision made. The plan forming vaguely in his mind was only a hope, dependent on more than a little luck. But it looked like the only hope he had.

Although the morning sun was bright, making the snowy expanse all around him a sea of diamonds whose glitter hurt the eyes, the air was still cold. He was glad he had been allowed to wear his jacket last night while he dug for gold on the roof of the soddy. Nevertheless, within minutes after he left the shack he found himself sweating under the jacket. He labored up a gentle slope that had appeared to be an easy climb as he started upward. His legs were soon wobbly and the pain in his side became a steady throbbing. The shock of a bullet tearing flesh away, even when the blow was not fatal or even very deep, was still not something the body recovered from overnight.

Ramon Sanudo had known. He had been right, Garrison admitted reluctantly. If he was to make his play at all, he had had to do it alone.

Garrison reached the trees and followed the Mexican's trail through them, his glance probing the surrounding area for what he was searching for. At the same time he remained alert for any movement ahead of him. Whenever the contours of the snow-covered land brought him to a rise, or when a seam or gully opened out to the north and he was able to glimpse the threadlike line of the stream that cut a path along the length of the valley, he stopped to study the white expanse below for any riders.

Not yet.

The delay bothered him. He became more uneasy about the fresh trail he followed. He plodded forward more slowly, squinting against the blinding glare.

A fall of rocks gave him the chance he had been hoping for. They shouldered above the surrounding terrain, forming a broken step exposed to the wind. Most of the surface of the formation had been swept clean of snow. Garrison would leave no tracks among those rocks.

He had to jump when he left the trail, for he wanted no sign to indicate what he had done. Behind him was only a single line of footsteps, for he had kept as much as possible to the tracks of Ramon Sanudo's horse. A careful tracker would quickly see through the ruse—but maybe not quickly enough.

Garrison clambered over the rocky step for perhaps twenty yards in search of a niche large enough to conceal him. There he found it. It was a break between two huge boulders, forming a shallow trough where a man might lie unseen but still be able to watch the trail to the west.

As he eased down and flattened out, Garrison glanced along the line of horse tracks. A hundred yards away, a horse and rider stepped around a bend and pulled up.

It was the shot Garrison had gambled on, a clear shot against a man who had not yet seen him and sat motionless. Garrison quickly brought the carbine to his shoulder and sighted along the barrel.

For an instant he hesitated. The man he saw was Dandy, and he appeared to be alone. Perhaps it was because Garrison was waiting to see if there was another rider that his trigger finger stayed. Or maybe it was only that it went against his grain to shoot a man from ambush without warning. Whatever the reason, he waited too long.

Suddenly the easy target was gone. Dandy threw himself off his horse. The piebald bolted in surprise. The little gunman hit the snow, rolled, and vanished behind a tangle of brush. Garrison's belated shot kicked up a spurt of snow where he had been.

He had had his brief chance because the sun was in Dandy's eyes, making the snow glare worse, half blinding him. The snow was at Garrison's back as he had planned, giving him a better view. But the sun had also worked against him. Too late he was aware of the glitter of light along the barrel of the carbine.

Garrison swore softly. It was the kind of mistake a man didn't often get to make a second time.

The space between him and Dandy was relatively flat, with a scattering of trees and low brush. Neither man could move far across that open without being seen.

Garrison glanced at Dandy's mare. She had run over part of the distance between the two men and was now slowly drifting closer to Garrison. She was still fifty or sixty yards away. Peering at the horse, Garrison saw the stock of a rifle protruding above its leather sling.

He had one advantage, then. Dandy had not had time to snake his rifle out before he jumped from his horse. He had his six-gun, but at this distance Garrison had the advantage.

He had to keep Dandy off. If the slick little gunfighter was able to get close, the tables would be turned. Dandy could move faster than Garrison. Dandy could shoot faster, and at close range he wouldn't have to worry as much about aiming.

Glimpsing a stir of movement, Garrison placed a shot directly ahead of the shadow. It stopped moving.

Dandy lifted into view long enough to snap off a single shot, but he was down again before Garrison could return the fire. He wasn't much worried about being hit with that kind of gunfire, but by the same token he had little chance of dropping the gunman.

It was a standoff.

Silence settled over the scene. Dandy did not reappear. Squinting, Garrison thought he could see a patch of darkness that wasn't natural, hardly more than a shadow behind some snow-covered rocks, but he wasn't sure and he didn't waste another shot. The interval of silence lengthened, became a minute, two minutes. . . .

He began to worry. He could see nothing moving, but instinct told him that he was in trouble. Dandy was not the kind to let himself be pinned down for long without taking action. He was not a patient sort, and he fancied himself as a fighter. The problem was, having lost sight of Dandy—having let him get away once when he could have been taken easily—Garrison was now the one who was pinned down among his rocks. He had good enough cover but only as long as he knew where his enemy was. Dandy could be anywhere, working closer, circling off to either side to find better cover, using the rolls and dips of the land to conceal his movement. He wasn't hurt and he could move quickly. This meadow, for instance, seemed to end abruptly—

Something caught Garrison's eye. He stared hard off to his left where the flat meadow dropped away. He thought he had seen a faint drift of white powder, as if something had disturbed the fine snow. Now it was gone. Or had he only imagined it?

There was a dip in the land at the edge of the meadow, its contours hidden by the snow. How deep was that depression? Could it hide a man?

For a full minute Garrison watched that clean edge of snow, his eyes straining until they watered from the glare. He blinked and shook his head. Then he peered again toward the crease.

Another faint puff, like fine smoke, appeared. It quickly vanished as the snow was caught by a light breeze.

Dandy was working toward him along that shallow depression.

Garrison knew that he had to move. He could no longer stay on his pan of rock while Dandy closed in on him. At the same time, as soon as he left his cover Dandy would gain another kind of advantage, for Garrison moved in pain, awkwardly and stiffly.

From the corner of his eye he glimpsed Dandy's mare,

drifting a little closer to him as she searched vainly for bare patches in the snow.

Garrison stared hard at the piebald, his mind working quickly.

After a moment he eased off the flat rock on which he lay and slid behind the barrier. The step was waist high, and he dropped into a low crouch as he struggled through deep snow back toward the trail he had been following. Mindful of the warning sign he had glimpsed of Dandy's movements, he tried not to kick up any snow. He guessed that the gunfighter was on his belly, crawling along a shallow crease not deep enough to hide the white dust he stirred up. Garrison could only hope that his rock cover—and the fact that Dandy was still looking somewhat into the sun—would conceal his own dust.

From the trail he squinted toward the meadow's edge where he had last placed the gunman. Garrison tracked along the path Dandy was following. When he spotted what looked like another drift of powder, it was much closer than he had expected. Dandy was closing in on Garrison's last position in the rocks much too quickly. He had to be slowed down a little.

Garrison sent a shot off across the open. He didn't place the bullet across Dandy's path but far behind him, at the spot where the gunfighter had tumbled from his horse to take cover. The crack of the rifle was echoed by the duller thud of the bullet hammering into the trunk of a tree Garrison had aimed at.

Garrison permitted himself a grim smile. The fine drift of powder that marked Dandy's movement was suddenly gone. The shot would not hold him long—it had been meant to give him a reason to pause. And it was intended to give him confidence that Garrison didn't know where he was. An overconfident man wouldn't be thinking of other possibilities.

Sucking in a breath, Garrison broke into a hard run. He

had to force his legs to keep driving through knee-deep snow, and he resisted the impulse to keep looking over his shoulder. Dandy's horse was only twenty yards away now, but each jarring step drove pain through Garrison's side, jolting the breath from him. The mare looked up as he came near. She backed off a step, uncertain. If only she didn't shy . . .

Garrison reached the horse and pulled up, gasping for breath. He looked across the open meadow. Dandy hadn't heard him. He wasn't in sight.

Garrison stepped around the mare, smacked her hard across the flank and yelled, "Aiyeeee—git!"

The piebald took off at a gallop. Garrison dropped to one knee. He caught a flying clod of snow across the mouth. He shook his head and spat. In the same moment he brought the carbine to his shoulder.

Dandy jumped into sight. Even across a span of thirty yards the alarm was clearly visible on his face. For an instant his gaze was on the running horse. Too late he saw Garrison kneeling.

Garrison did not hesitate this time. He squeezed off a careful shot.

When Dandy fired back, for a moment Garrison thought that, incredibly, he had missed. But Dandy's shot went wild, and then he was stumbling around, trying to stay on his feet. Garrison's second shot cut him down.

Garrison eased slowly to his feet. The gunsmoke blew away. Snow spray settled around the gunman's body. He did not move. Silence once more settled over the meadow, and Garrison took in a long, slow breath, letting the hammering excitement in his chest slow to a canter.

He stared back along Dandy's trail then, which had earlier been Ramon Sanudo's trail. Garrison had taken one long risk he could not escape, but now he knew that he had been lucky.

Dandy had come alone.

CHAPTER 8

～ 1 ～

Early that morning, the town of Cedar Point had a bleak, abandoned look. Snow was knee-deep over most of the single main street, much higher in the alleys and wherever drifts had piled against buildings. But there were signs that the town was alive. The snow was trampled into hard-pack where horses had trod, and there were broad furrows to mark the passage of wagon wheels. Some of the boardwalk had been kept clear of snow. There was little of it in front of the Silver Palace or the Copper Kettle Cafe. The porch of the hotel was clean. Two chairs remained on the porch, unoccupied, gestures toward a warmer time.

As the day came on there was activity. A rider plodded east alone, huddled inside a thick sheepskin coat, leaving town with what seemed little enthusiasm for his journey. A wagon rolled into town, stopping at the general store. Other stores opened their doors, more out of habit than in anticipation of any business. A drummer came out onto the porch of the hotel to stare along the quiet street with an expression of disgust.

Pegleg Parks plodded into view shortly before noon. In spite of the snow he managed to get around the small town surprisingly well on his crutches. He hated being cooped up, and this winter had the look and feel of a long, hard season.

Parks stayed indoors when the weather was particularly bad. The cold got into his bones, especially his recently shattered leg. And he wasn't very steady on his crutches in a high wind or when the footing iced over. Then he felt something like a rickety, top-heavy windmill with the wind whistling around his crutches. But when the weather turned, as it did this morning, he was eager to feel the sun.

For ten cents a night he had been sleeping on a bunk in the converted stables behind the Bauers' rooming house. Irene Bauer was a close woman with a dollar, and this makeshift bunkhouse—which Pegleg Parks shared with a half dozen other winter-broke regulars and an occasional transient rider—was sparsely furnished, containing little more than crudely framed wooden bunks with thin straw mats. Behind each bed was a board nailed to the wall to form a shelf, where you could deposit any personal effects too worthless to be stolen. Parks couldn't afford a decent bed in the rooming house itself, or regular meals there, for that matter. Like others who were down to their last chip, he was glad enough simply to get out of the wind. Even in a place where the blankets seemed to have a life of their own.

Parks spent little time these days in the Silver Palace. He knew he had to nurse the dwindling remains of his fall wages—he still owed the doctor for treatment of his leg. If Virgil Pryor didn't return soon, Pegleg was going to be scraping the blanket all too quickly. Pryor didn't pay him in winter. There was little for a hand to do, and Pryor had made it plain that food and shelter were all Parks could expect if he stayed on at the ranch during these bitter months. But surely, Pegleg told himself, Pryor would advance him a little against his spring wages, enough to pay the doctor's bill and to enable him to buy a drink now and then to warm his belly on a cold night.

Most of the time Pegleg hung around the livery stables. Lester Cruikshank, who owned the livery barn, was an old friend. He was also a talkative man who liked to gossip and needed someone around to listen. Since everyone who came or went through Cedar Point put up his horse at Lester's stables, he was in a way to know most of what went on in town.

When this day emerged bright and clear, the sun sparkling off the fresh snow and bringing its touch of warmth to aching bones, Pegleg hobbled along the street until he came to the stables at the west end of town. It was hard work getting there, and he was glad to drop onto a bench in the shed where Lester had his blacksmith's forge. Cruikshank was hammering some horseshoes into shape. The heat from the forge was delicious, a solid wall of heat that tightened Pegleg's skin and soon had him feeling baked through.

In between hammer blows Lester talked about the weather, a fight that had broken up a table and a half-dozen chairs in the Silver Palace last night, and the comings and goings of various people. Finally he glanced up in a moment of ringing silence and inquired, "What did your boss have to say about you bustin' up your good leg?"

"Ain't seen him," Pegleg Parks said, surprised by the question. "Been two months or so since he left, maybe more." Weeks and months had a way of running into each other, especially in winter.

"He's been around, what I hear."

"That can't be. I'da seen him."

"Pete Johnson said he saw Virgil the other day, over by his spread. Not close enough to holler so he could've been mistaken, but Pete give him a wave, he said, and Pryor waved back. He was on the old wagon road that comes down from Fort Belknap. Pete wondered if maybe Pryor hadn't come as far as the fort on the train and rode south from there."

"Did you put his horse up? You'd know if he's been in town."

"Well, I never said I seen him myself. But Raymond Soule was sayin' he thought Virgil was back." Cruikshank paused once more in his labors. "Did Pryor ever say where he goes off to, Pegleg?"

"You know Virgil don't talk much about hisself." Troubled, Pegleg added, "You sure it was him Pete Johnson seen? If'n Virgil had heard about my leg, he would surely have looked me up, you'd expect."

Lester Cruikshank held up a shoe for inspection, gave it a couple more artistic bangs with his hammer and, satisfied, dipped the shoe into a pail of water. Over the hissing of steam Lester said, "Well, now, you'd think so, Pegleg, but you can't never tell about Virgil Pryor. He ain't what you'd call a predictable man."

"No . . ." The more Pegleg thought about it, the more disturbed he became. He had wanted to talk to Pryor as soon as possible. Wanted him to know that he would be on his feet again long before winter stopped howling. Doc Hibbs said his leg was healing fine. Hell, he could stand a buckboard ride right now. He could heal at the ranch as fast as he could here in town. Anyway, ever since he'd talked to that drifter a couple of days ago, Pegleg had been bothered about Pryor's missus being left alone at the ranch. (He thought too much of Trish to admit openly that she was not properly married to Pryor.) "By God, Lester, I got to get out there."

"You ain't in no shape to ride yet."

"I could handle a buckboard," the gimpy little cowhand answered stubbornly. "You must have a rig around that I could borrow."

"What would you do if you was to get bogged down?"

Cruikshank said dubiously. "You'd be breakin' trail the whole way. That's deep snow, Pegleg. Might be you should wait a spell longer." Then, as if he too had just remembered the pretty blond girl who had been a favorite listener of his own when she was growing up in town, he asked, "How's that little woman of Virgil's gettin' along? Seems like I haven't seen her since summer."

Pegleg hesitated. He had his own opinion of the way Virgil Pryor sometimes treated his woman. But Lester Cruikshank liked to gossip too much. "I reckon she gets fidgety with Virgil away so long. She oughtn't to be there alone."

"It don't seem proper. . . ." Lester caught himself, glanced around the stables nervously like a superstitious man looking for a ghost, and shivered. Hastily he amended what he had been about to say. "Bad luck you and that Mex both bein' away."

"I got to get out there, Lester."

"Well . . . Pete Johnson's boy stayed over in town. Little Pete's a big, strong lad. Maybe you could talk him into drivin' you out to Pryor's place. If anyone could cut a trail through, I reckon Little Pete might do it."

Pegleg Parks seized upon the suggestion eagerly. Thanking Lester, who agreed to lend him the use of a beat-up wagon left behind by the widow Mitchell when she went back East after Barney Mitchell passed away in September, Pegleg made his tortured way back along the street. After several stops he found Little Pete Johnson in the Copper Kettle wolfing down a plate of roast beef and potatoes that seemed ample enough to feed a crew of hungry ranch hands. An easygoing youth, Little Pete—at eighteen he was already taller and wider than his father, although not yet as heavy—agreed to drive Pegleg out to the Pryor place. He had not planned to leave town for another day, however—he had "important business," he told Pegleg, with a sly grin. But they might be able to set off early the next day.

Pegleg Parks trudged back to the livery stables to inform Lester Cruikshank of the arrangement. Lester agreed to hitch up the wagon in the morning. After some more desultory talk, Pegleg made his slow and painful way back to the bunkhouse behind the rooming house. He was fatigued by all of his activity, and the smell of meat and gravy while he was talking to Little Pete Johnson had made him somewhat queasy. His morning meal of canned tomatoes and stale bread was the only food he had eaten this day. Cooking smells from Irene Bauer's kitchen renewed the hunger pangs. He thought with longing of Trish Pryor's cooking, of beef and gravy and hot bread to wipe the plate with. . . .

Anxious to leave town as soon as possible, he fretted over having to stay another day because a young man's sap was running. The bunkhouse was empty, a cheerless, gloomy cavern even in the bright of day. Until the prospect of a quick return to the Pryor ranch beckoned, Pegleg had not admitted to himself how bleak and aimless the time in town had been since his accident, how long the days, how cold and uninviting this place where he slept. Not that the corner of the Pryor barn that served as bunkhouse for him and Ramon was any palace. But Pegleg felt different being there. He didn't own it, there was nothing that he could really call his own, but he belonged there. Everything was familiar, even the smells of leather and horses and stored grain, the soft cooing of doves high in the loft, the gold of the light in the early morning. And he had a job, a purpose. Even in winter, when there were few regular chores, he could always find gear to fix, harnesses to mend, a worn saddle blanket to patch.

A thought, sudden and terrifying, made him sit up on

his bunk. The thought had been with him, hidden from himself by a curtain of fear, since the moment he felt the bones in his leg give way when he was crushed against the side of the barn. The thought that he might be finished, less useful than an old harness that could be repaired and made as good as new. The fear had been there with the terrible pain when he lay in the wagon as Trish Lovell drove him into town to the doctor, the thought that he might not come back this way. . . .

He was sitting up, sweating and trembling, when the door at the end of the bunkhouse opened.

The door closed quickly, and for a moment Pegleg was not sure of his eyesight. Then the man who had entered the dark room spoke and he recognized Virgil Pryor's voice. "I heard about your trouble, Pegleg," Pryor said. He didn't make it sound like real trouble. "Cruikshank said I might find you here."

"Mr. Pryor! I'm right glad to see you!"

Pryor came over to stand beside Pegleg's bunk. He was wearing a long black coat and nearly new black boots. Both coat and boots seemed spotless, as if he had walked on top of the snow and any that fell around him was sure to miss him. He nodded at the pair of crutches leaning against the wall beside the bunk. "Must be hard to drag yourself around on sticks like that."

"You get used to it," Pegleg said quickly. "I'm gettin' right handy with these."

Pryor thoughtfully began to remove his leather gloves. He plucked at the tips of the fingers one by one, smoothed the leather out, and folded the gloves carefully before he put them in a pocket of his coat. "Let's see now," he drawled, "you only had one good leg before. I reckon now it won't be worth much."

Pegleg flushed. "I'll be able to get around." He was going to stand up, as if to demonstrate his agility with the crutches, but Pryor was crowding so close that the little cowhand sank back onto the bunk. "You'll see, Mr. Pryor. Hell, a hand don't need to be quick afoot once he's in the saddle. Don't you worry about me. I'll be fit as ever by greenup."

"I don't rightly see how I'd have much use for a hand who couldn't fall out of the saddle by his lonesome," Pryor said amiably.

"Huh?" Pegleg Parks stared up at Pryor, perplexed, unable—or unwilling—to see where Pryor's comment was leading. "I never needed no helping hand, Mr. Pryor. You know that. No sirree. I allus worked for my wages," he added defensively. No allowance had ever been given for his shortened leg, and he had never asked for any. It was a matter of pride with him. Not that Pryor had ever paid much, or been an easy man to work for. Pegleg felt that he had given more than his due, and Pryor knew it.

"I need a hand to round up cattle and wrestle a calf for branding. Takes an able-bodied man."

Pegleg Parks bristled indignantly. "I can ride and rope as good as any man! And I can—"

"But you can't keep from breakin' your bones. You can't stay put where you're supposed to. I can't count on you to look after Mrs. Pryor when I'm gone." Pryor smiled deceptively—that friendly, careless grin that might deceive you into thinking he was an easy man. "Lester Cruikshank told me you was planning to ride out to my place. There's no need for that. You just rest up here in town." He spoke softly, but when Pegleg started to protest, Pryor silenced him with an upraised palm. "You aren't listening good, Pegleg. Point is, I don't want to see you on my place. It isn't a home for cripples."

The words brought a chill to Pegleg Parks' heart. "That's a . . . a mean thing to say to any man," he protested weakly.

Something flared in Virgil Pryor's eyes that deepened the chill enveloping the old man. His heart seemed to shrivel in his chest, making it hard for him to breathe.

Still smiling, Pryor lashed out suddenly with the back of his hand. It caught Parks across the side of the face. He spilled over backward and had to grab the edge of the bunk to keep from falling to the floor. He lay on his back, trembling, his broken leg hurting from the awkward tumble.

Virgil Pryor said, "I give you that one say, old man. Don't crowd your luck no more. I reckon folks wouldn't take it right if I was to finish you off here and now, an old cripple like you. But that doesn't mean you can't hurt a hell of a lot worse than you do now."

Pegleg Parks said nothing. He had seen Virgil Pryor angry. The blow he had just taken was a little love tap compared to what he might face if he made Pryor really angry. Pegleg lay on his bunk, shaking and hurting, saying nothing. Even when he thought of telling Pryor about the drifter, Garrison, as he had intended, he was silent. That news, if Pryor didn't already know of it, might only make him more dangerous.

After a long moment Pryor turned and walked out without a backward glance. Long after the door had closed behind him the old man continued to lie on his back in the dark, cold room. As his fright subsided slowly, questions began to surface like rocks emerging from a receding pool. Where had Pryor been these past months? When had he returned? If it was true that Pete Johnson had seen him two days ago, around the time the last big storm hit, where had Pryor been for two days? At the ranch? Holed up here in town? But why was he making himself so scarce? And why had he suddenly decided he didn't want Parks going out to his place in the morning?

Pegleg had left the ranch in too much of a hurry and in no condition to collect the few personal belongings he kept stashed under his bunk in a corner of the barn as if they had real value, those geegaws a cowboy gave space in his warbag, reluctant for one reason or another to throw them away. He had thought of them before Pryor left but had been afraid to speak up. He had left nothing behind that was worth crossing Pryor for. Besides, Pegleg knew, as clearly as he had ever perceived anything in his life, that he would not dare to set foot on Pryor's land again, whatever the reason. He wasn't wanted there.

And Virgil Pryor never gave a second warning.

 2

As the sun climbed higher and then tilted over toward the west Staggs became increasingly restless, his nerves on edge. He kept prowling back and forth in the soddy's close quarters. He would go to the window and stare out for a long time, then swing back to glower at Trish Lovell as if she were somehow to blame for his frustration. He would make up another cigarette, swearing when he spilled tobacco, light it and after only a few puffs throw it half smoked into the fire. Sometimes he stepped to the door for a longer survey of the snow-bright land. And he would talk to himself. "Where the hell is he? He should have been back long before this. What's takin' him so long?"

The silence in itself was an answer, but it was one he was not ready to admit.

When day broke there had been three of them. Now Cullen lay cold under a blanket of snow, killed by a crazy

Mexican trying to pull off a foolhardy stunt no one could have expected.

And Dandy had been gone for nearly four hours.

Three hours since Staggs had heard the distant rattle of gunfire. There had been a number of shots, with different weight to the sounds. More than one gun had been fired, and the meaning of that was plain. Dandy had not encountered a wounded, helpless man, unable to shoot back.

But where was Dandy now? Staggs could not bring himself to accept what reason told him. Dandy was both snake-quick and deadly accurate with rifle or six-shooter. When he went up against a no-account drifter like Garrison, already half dead, the outcome was foregone. It shouldn't even have been a fight.

Reluctantly Staggs came to accept one possibility: They had underestimated Garrison. He was tricky. And like any wounded animal, most dangerous when he was hurt and desperate. He might have gotten in his licks before Dandy sent him on his way to drifters' hell. That would explain why Dandy hadn't returned. He could be lying out there, hit, waiting for help.

Staggs thought about saddling up and riding after him, but the prospect awakened no enthusiasm. It would mean leaving the woman alone or taking her with him. The latter course would put him into a bind if he ran into trouble. He could tie her up in the soddy for safekeeping, but even that would involve a risk he didn't like. It would mean leaving the house unguarded.

The possibility that he didn't want to admit—that Garrison, not Dandy, might have survived the exchange of gunfire—ruled out leaving the soddy. Staggs didn't want to be the one on the outside, with Garrison and the woman forted up in the house. They might be able to hold out indefinitely. There was enough food here to get by on, plenty of water, firewood to keep the place warm.

No. Staggs was not going to abandon all that. Dandy was on his own.

Time passed. As the afternoon crawled on, Staggs became more sullen, given to long periods of sitting motionless in brooding silence.

Trish Lovell had watched the gradual change in his mood. She stayed out of Staggs' way, doing nothing to antagonize him. A numbness had settled over her, a deadening of her feelings that brought back with awful vividness the time so many years ago when she huddled shivering on a riverbank while the Comanche raiders celebrated their attack against the wagon train. Her mind kept wanting to go back to the moment when Cullen swung the shovel at Ramon Sanudo, but each time she flinched away from the memory.

She wondered if Garrison also was dead.

Staggs rose suddenly, breaking a long stillness. "Goddamn sonuvabitch!" he swore.

Trish felt her heart racing. His abrupt explosion had startled her. "It isn't his doing," she said. "You forced all this on Mr. Garrison. He was only passing through—"

"Not him!" Staggs glared at her. "I mean Pryor. He brought this all on! You picked a fine one to shack up with. Or maybe you didn't know he was a murderin' thief and a double-crosser to boot."

Trish Lovell flushed. She hadn't known. She had been too quick to accept a smiling face as the real image of the man behind it, too eager to yield to the tingling excitement he had awakened in her. Once she had become Virgil Pryor's woman, she had soon enough found herself on an emotional teeter-totter, the high moments of excited happiness more than balanced by ugly incidents that chipped away at her childish illusions. But that had been a private shame. She had still been naïve enough about Virgil Pryor to be shocked by the discovery that he was both thief and murderer. She now no longer questioned Staggs' description of Pryor. It answered many questions she had ignored, unwilling to pursue them. She had never even seriously dared to question where and how he came by the periodic windfalls that filled his pockets with the money he would then spend so freely. . . .

There was a great deal about Virgil Pryor she hadn't known.

"How did you come to fall in with him—Virgil, I mean?"

"It wasn't my lucky day," Staggs answered sullenly. She thought he was going to ignore her question, but after a moment he said, "I saw him cut down this poor dumb bastard up in Abilene. A cowboy, that's all he was, but he thought he was meaner than an alligator. He was in a card game with Virgil and the cowboy lost big. I reckon it was the end of the trail north for him and he'd jest collected his pay and he saw it all goin' into somebody else's pockets, somebody who never even got dirty doin' it, who never sweated or ate dust or rode on an empty belly. Maybe he couldn't take losin', or maybe it was true that Virgil was dealin' from the bottom—you can't never tell with Virg. He'd never say, not even afterward. That's a thing you got to understand about ol' Virg: He don't let you know anythin' he don't want you to know. He's always thinkin' ahead, figgerin' out how you might be able to use somethin' against him or how he could maybe use it against you." Staggs paused, reminiscing. Then he said, softly, "That dumb cowboy called Virgil down, said he was cheatin' him, markin' the deck. Virgil kinda smiled at him and let him talk. Everybody else in this saloon scattered, gettin' out of the way. I was there at the bar, watchin', and I never moved. I never seen Virgil Pryor before that day, but I *knew* what was gonna happen. Virgil let him talk a while, yellin' what he was gonna do to Virgil for cheatin' him. Finally Virg says, real quiet, 'You all done, peckerhead?' And the duster says he's just gettin' started. So Virg chuckles and shakes his head and he says, 'Wrong, peckerhead. You're finished.' And then Virgil stands up and tells him he can die talking or reachin' for iron, Virgil don't especially care which. There was jest a second or two, maybe, when that dumb cow nurse knew he'd made a mistake. But there wasn't nothin' he could do to change it. He'd gone too far and he couldn't back up. So he grabs for his gun and quick as a wink Virgil shoots him in the knee.

"Well, the cowboy drops his gun when he goes down, bawlin' like a calf feelin' the hot iron. Virgil goes over and kicks the gun out of the poor puncher's reach so he'll have to crawl over to get it. That's what Virgil tells him. 'Crawl, you peckerhead,' he says. He did it so's that cowhand couldn't get out of it. He couldn't jest lie there and figger he was lucky gettin' away with a busted leg. Virgil wouldn't let him, and there was too many of us watchin'. That dumb rider had to crawl after his gun. And Virgil let him get maybe inches away from it and then he shoots him in the other leg. Hit the knee both times. So now this cowboy is busted up in both legs and he knows he'll never walk again and he starts screamin' at Virgil and he grabs for that six-gun even though he has to know there's no way he'll ever have a chance. Virgil lets him get hold of it and then he finishes him off."

"Oh my God," Trish Lovell whispered, shuddering.

Staggs for the moment was lost in his memory of the incident. "That's when ol' Virg looks at me for the first time, right in the eye, and he says, 'He a friend of yours?' And I says, 'Hell, any friend of mine has more sense than that.' And Virgil stares at me for a minute, and then he nods and grins all of a sudden—I reckon you know that grin of his—like maybe we was long-lost brothers, and he says, 'Thirsty work, playin' cards. How about a drink?'"

Staggs was smiling as he finished the story. The smile faded slowly as he came back from that remembered time to the cold and bitter present. "That's how come we threw in together, me and Virgil. Cullen was ridin' with me then, and Dandy joined up later. . . ."

"Why did he do it?" Trish cried, wanting to reject what Staggs had recounted, yet unable to deny the ring of truth in the story. "That poor man . . . why?"

"Virgil likes to hurt people," Staggs answered with a shrug. It was not a judgment but a simple statement of fact, tinged perhaps with something of admiration. "You oughta know that, ma'am, bein' as you're his woman."

His woman. She felt a sudden loathing, not so much for Virgil Pryor as for herself. It was only a little over a year ago, at the end of summer, when Pryor had brought her to this house to stay as his woman. Shortly afterward he had gone North "on business." Now she knew where his business had taken him. To Abilene.

After a while she said, "Why don't you leave, Mr. Staggs? There's no money here. Don't you see that now? What have you to stay for?"

Staggs glared at her. "Pryor will come back. He has to."

"Do you really want him to find you here? Do you want to end up like that poor cowhand?"

The comment goaded Staggs into an angry eruption. "Shut up! My spine don't turn to taffy when you throw his name at me. Yeah, I *want* him to come!"

His anger encouraged her. He was afraid, she thought. Fear lurked behind the blustering words. "If there is any money, he'll never let you near it. He'll kill you first."

"Maybe I've got somethin' belongs to him that'll

change his mind. You seem to be forgettin' that." Staggs paused, his nasty grin reappearing. "I've got *you*."

She was silent for a long time. When she answered it was with the quiet acceptance of a woman facing a bitter truth. "That won't help you," she said.

 3

Dave Garrison was angry, and the object of his rage was Virgil Pryor. Garrison was, to tell the truth, angry with himself, with Dandy, with Staggs and Cullen as well as Pryor, but it was easier to divert all that anger toward a specific target. Pryor, after all, was ultimately to blame for Garrison having to kill a man to save his own skin. Pryor could be held to account for any more killing as well—as far as Garrison knew there were still two of Pryor's former sidekicks waiting for him. Pryor was also the reason Garrison felt a jolt of pain with every step taken by Dandy's mare, which he was now riding slowly in the direction of Pryor's ranch buildings. During the ride Garrison felt the wound in his side open up again. The bandage Ramon Sanudo had applied was soaked through.

Finally, the only reason Garrison couldn't simply turn Dandy's mare around and ride off in the other direction was the fact that Patricia Lovell was being held by Staggs and Cullen. And she wasn't his woman to protect. She was Virgil Pryor's woman.

Dave Garrison was not a brawler—he had the contempt shared by most of his kind for punching heads with his fists. But it was also true—again like most of his kind—that he wouldn't back away from a fight that was forced on him, or that seemed necessary. During the War Between the States, for instance, or later on when he signed on as a scout with the Army in Arizona Territory, he had accepted the need to use a gun against other men. But Garrison had never sought out a fight without reason. Moreover, he had never before gone into one that, from any reasonable point of view, could only be regarded as foolhardy.

By nature Garrison was a loner. He enjoyed the good-humored give-and-take of other men like himself, men with whom he had shared the dust of a cattle drive, the tingling excitement of an Indian raid, or the still moments that often came at night by a campfire, a pinpoint of light in the vast darkness of the plains. But in the way of loners he had always drifted on, going his own way. If someone pushed him too hard, he would dig in his heels, but it was his own stubborn pride that found the digging point. The battles he fought were his own, the choice to stay or go his own. All of his baggage could be tied up in a fairly efficient bedroll. In it could be found no extra cargo of debts unpaid—or responsibilities for someone else. Garrison had never wanted it any other way.

Or so he told himself, feeding his anger during the painful ride from the meadow where he had left Dandy in the snow. Now here he was sticking his neck out for a woman he hadn't seen in eight years and who was then a child. And who now belonged to another man.

He was angry with Pryor for going off and leaving Trish Lovell alone. If he had buried gold somewhere on his land, Pryor must surely have known that the partners he had double-crossed would sooner or later track him down. Garrison did not burn with any sudden gold fever. He didn't give a damn about the stolen money. That was between Pryor and Staggs and the others. The gold was Pryor's until someone took it away from him, the woman was Pryor's, the fight was his.

Even Ramon Sanudo came in for a share of Garrison's

anger. The Mexican had worked for Pryor but it was obvious that he had felt more loyalty toward the man Pryor
had taken the land from. Still, he had unhesitatingly
taken on an unequal fight against three men. The fight
had not been Ramon's either, but he had not hesitated to
deal himself in. Smiling, he had gone off on his romantic
mission alone. Garrison wondered, his anger turning sour,
if Ramon had still been smiling when he died.

There was no doubt in Garrison's mind that Ramon
had lost his final play in the game. Otherwise Dandy
would not have been backtracking along the Mexican's
trail.

A quarter mile south of the Pryor soddy, hidden from it
by a brush-topped knoll, Garrison climbed painfully
down from Dandy's mare. From the crest of the rise,
careful to keep some of the winter-ragged brush behind
him so that he was not skylined, Garrison studied the
scene below him.

There was no activity. Whoever was still there was inside the house. Or in the barn. Garrison could not ignore
the latter possibility. Staggs might have sent Cullen out
to the barn, on the chance that there might be others like
Ramon coming to rescue the fair maiden. Others as smiling and foolish and brave.

Smoke from the chimney was the only sign of life.
While he watched and waited, Garrison's anger slowly
drained away, as the sickness that came from killing a
man began to recede. Dandy had deserved killing, but
that never made it easy.

Finally he decided that he had to have a closer look.
He had to find out exactly what he was up against.

The more he thought about the possible presence of a
sentinel in the barn, the more logical that notion
sounded. If he had been in Staggs' boots he would have
taken such a precaution. Someone in the barn could

watch the house, making sure that no one sneaked up behind it. He could also detect any approach from the east along the valley floor. And having Cullen in the barn would deny Garrison the shelter offered there—even the warmth of the horses' bodies if the day turned colder.

Of course, one sentry couldn't look both ways at the same time. And there would be only one in the barn. Staggs himself was probably in the house. He wouldn't leave the woman alone there. What Garrison had to do, if he was going to check out his hunch, was create a diversion. He had to be sure the sentry was looking in the wrong direction.

He weighed a number of ruses before he thought of the simplest one. He went back down the slope to retrieve Dandy's mare from the small grove of trees where he had tethered her. She was restless, knowing that she was close to human habitation. Garrison was certain that all he had to do was turn her loose and she would head straight for the barn.

He led her close to the top of the knoll, following Dandy's earlier tracks. There he gave her a sharp slap on the flank as he released her. She jumped away from the slap, hesitated only a moment until she knew she was free, and immediately picked up the morning trail. From the brow of the knoll Garrison watched her trotting briskly toward the cluster of buildings below.

He did not wait to see what happened next. He set off in a floundering run, trying to judge the uneven drifts as he broke a new path through the snow. It was heavy going. He had to make a wide circle to be sure of keeping out of sight before he began to work in toward the barn, being careful to keep it always between himself and the house as he drew closer to the buildings. At one point he caught a glimpse of the mare in the open yard between the house and barn. After that he could not see what was going on out front, but he was sure that anyone posted as a watch in the barn would have his eyes on the mare and the track she had followed. He wouldn't be looking toward the rear of the barn.

There was a back door but it was almost completely hidden by the deep drifts that had piled up against the wall. There was no way to get at the door quickly. The drifts rose above Garrison's head almost to the bottom of a pair of wooden shutters that covered an opening to a loft. When Garrison tried to climb up this soft slope to reach the loft window, he sank into snow to his waist. Halfway up he could go no farther.

Stumbling clear of the drift, he tripped over a pile of loose boards stacked close to the end wall of the building. Working quickly, he pulled a long, wide board free of the snow. He laid it along the slope of the drift, angled upward toward the loft window.

He went up the board gingerly, using his hands and feet like a monkey climbing a tree. The flat surface of the board sank a few inches under his weight before it held.

Near the top he paused. The board had not taken him quite as high as he had hoped. Carefully he rose to his feet. He reached up. Stretching, he was able to grip the sill of the window.

The shutters were loose, held in place only because they were both unevenly warped. He edged one flap open. He drew himself up until he could peer over the edge.

It took a moment for his eyes to adjust to the dimness inside the barn. His arms quivered from the strain. He saw that the loft was empty except for a little straw piled along one side. There were a couple of broken boards in the loft floor through which he could see a glimpse of the area below. Something moved. Garrison froze into stillness. Staying motionless always offered a better chance to escape being seen than any sudden movement. Then a horse nickered softly. Garrison let out a long, frosty breath.

The next part was both awkward and risky. He let himself down until one foot found the end of the board. Then he retrieved Ramon's rifle, which he had stacked against the barn wall. He was able to slide the rifle through the window opening. When he dragged the shutter all the way open, far enough to allow him to climb through, it grated as it rubbed over the sill.

Once that noise was made Garrison moved as fast as he could. Shutting off any concern for the sharp tug he felt at his side, he got both hands over the windowsill, then an elbow. He heaved upward. He slithered through the opening head first and dropped to the floor of the loft.

Grabbing the rifle, Garrison scurried to his right, away from the window, hoping there were no other broken or weak boards in the floor. Once into a corner, buffered by the layer of straw, he waited.

Over his own heavy heartbeat he could hear the horses stirring around below, sensing his presence, perhaps also aware of the arrival of the mare outside. Garrison let several minutes drag by before he accepted the probability that no one else was in the barn. His clumsy entry would surely have drawn fire from a sentinel.

When this guess became conviction, he climbed down from the loft and completed a search of the areas of the barn he had been unable to see from the loft. The horses in the barn—his own chestnut as well as others belonging to Staggs and Cullen and three presumably of Pryor's string—reacted eagerly. Guessing that they were more thirsty than hungry, Garrison looked around for and found a water barrel. He broke a thin layer of ice that had crusted over the top. Without the thought that he was doing anything unusual, he took the time to water each of the horses. In any event, he was no longer in a hurry. His adversaries had the house, he had the barn. And he had the advantage that they did not know he was there. He could take the time he needed to scout the situation further.

Through a crack in the front wall of the barn, he watched the house patiently. He thought he saw someone at the window but could not be sure who it was. It might have been Trish Lovell, and the thought quickened his heartbeat in a strange way, as if he had been running. After a while, when he was studying the area around the house and the hill into which it was set, something caught his eye. At first he didn't know what it was. Then he realized that the snow had clumped in an unnatural way on the south side of the soddy. Not in the familiar smooth sculpture wrought by wind but deliberately piled into some kind of a mound.

Garrison felt a prickling intuition. He thought he knew what was hidden under that freshly molded mound of snow. But he had to be certain.

He left the barn the way he had entered, through the loft window. He didn't try to climb down the board, which was still in place, but instead jumped into the deep, soft snowdrift.

Since he still had to keep away from any peephole at the front of the house, it took him a half hour to work his way completely around to the far side of the soddy, laboring sometimes through snow up to his thighs. Then he crept cautiously to the top of the rise that looked down on the soddy's slanting roof. He had little fear that Staggs or Cullen would plunge out of the safe cover of the house unexpectedly, but he didn't want to let them know where he was sooner than necessary.

He reached the mound on the south side of the house without incident. The snow was soft and loose where it had been hastily piled up. He had little difficulty pawing enough of it away to reveal what lay underneath.

He had expected to find Ramon Sanudo. Cullen was a surprise. Ramon had given as good as he received.

Garrison retreated behind the house once more. He was no longer blindly angry. Now he felt sadness—and a harsh, unrelenting purpose.

A cuplike drift near the top of the rise provided a rudimentary shelter where he could rest briefly. He was shivering, and he felt weakened by his exertions. He stared down at the roof of the soddy. A sudden shift in the light breeze carried smoke directly over him, stinging his eyes and nostrils. His body envied the touch of warmth.

Now he knew what he was up against. Now it was down to him and Staggs.

4

Dandy's long absence, and Staggs' worry, had revived a small hope to which Trish Lovell clung through the afternoon. She had believed Garrison dead, and it took a long time for grief to yield up this flickering new hope. When Staggs sullenly gave up his vigil at the window, she took his place. Staring out at the lonely length of the valley—the relentless snow, the winter-blasted cottonwoods that flanked the creek and the naked brush half buried by snow, the raw rock of the ridge thrusting upward to the north—had become a habit with her during her solitary days at the ranch. Sometimes she would look out for hours on end without expectation of seeing anything move. Tumbleweed blowing across the snow, leaving tracks like a flock of chickens, had been an event that held her transfixed.

She remembered how she had been looking out the day Garrison came—had it been only two days ago? How could so much have been packed into less than forty-eight hours, when so many days—even weeks—held nothing worth remembering? She remembered the ghost on the ridge, looking down at her through blowing snow. Not a ghost, of course. Nor a trick of the light. Nor, her calmer perspective told her now, a wolf.

"Were you spying on us, Mr. Staggs?" she murmured.

"What's that? What did you say?"

"The night Mr. Garrison came. It was you I saw up on that ridge, I reckon. That's how you knew he was here."

"I don't know what you're talking about," Staggs snarled. "We come that same night, if you're tellin' the truth about him, but we come down the valley."

She frowned, perplexed a little. Had it been Garrison then? She couldn't remember how long it was between the time she saw the ghost and the frightening pounding on her door.

While she stared up at the ridge, puzzled, a flash of movement caught her eye. She gasped. A horse cantered into view, slowing as it came near. A riderless horse, its saddle empty. A piebald with recognizable markings. "Mr. Staggs—look there!" she cried, hardly daring to believe what she saw.

Behind her Staggs swore viciously. "It can't be! I don't believe it! No drifter could put Dandy down."

She shuddered in relief at the confirmation. Her knees went weak and she put out a hand to catch the window-sill. The horse was Dandy's.

"Yeah, that's his mare, sure enough." He pushed her aside to stare through the window, his hard gaze darting along the fresh tracks the mare had left in the snow. "And she didn't run all the way back here on her own. It

ain't like this is her own barn, a place she'd know to come
back to. . . ."

Trish Lovell's relief became a quiet joy. Her hope
soared, mixed with wonder. Garrison was alive! Alive and
well enough to hold his own against the little gunman.
The mare's return, moreover, was not by chance. Staggs
was right. Garrison was sending Staggs—and her?—a mes-
sage. Garrison wanted Staggs to know that Dandy was
dead.

The word chilled her momentary elation. Dandy was
dead. Cullen and Ramon lay together beside the house.
Garrison himself had been wounded. There was nothing
in all this for her to celebrate. Nor any plausible reason to
believe that a wounded Garrison could accomplish more
than he already had. The odds were more even now—
Staggs, too, was now alone—but the outlaw was safe inside the house. He still held the upper hand. And he still
held her. . . .

She shivered, thinking of Garrison out there in the
cold, battered and bleeding. Safe and warm inside the
soddy, with food and water enough, Staggs could hold
out indefinitely. How long could Garrison carry on the
fight? What could he do?

"Get away from that window," Staggs ordered her. Not
waiting for her response, he shoved her roughly across
the room. Quickly he banged the shutters over the window and secured them. "Those stay shut, you hear? Garrison won't be throwing any lead into this room when he
can't see inside." His nasty, mirthless smile reappeared.
"He won't shoot when he can't see just who he might be
ventilating."

Acting purposefully now, the long period of waiting
and uncertainty over, Staggs dropped the bar across the
door, where it fitted snugly into a pair of heavy iron
braces, one on either side of the door. "It's cold out there.

And it's gonna be a colder night. Let's see how long Garrison can go without freezing." He scowled. "Dandy got careless. He was good, but sometimes that can make you careless. He didn't think he had to worry about Garrison. I'm not makin' the same mistake."

He gathered his stock of weapons on the wooden table and began to examine them, making sure that each was loaded. It was a formidable arsenal, including Trish's own rifle as well as weapons belonging to Cullen and Ramon Sanudo and Staggs himself.

Watching him, Trish Lovell felt her brief elation wither away. Staggs had been the leader of his crew. That told her that he was more dangerous than the huge but slow-witted Cullen, more deadly even than Dandy.

Staggs looked at her. "You been standin' around long enough. Put some more wood on that fire. Then I reckon it's time you started cookin' up somethin' for supper. Might be we got a long wait before this night is done."

He sounded, she thought with sinking hope, eager for what lay ahead.

CHAPTER 9

1

It was dusk when Garrison came. They heard him overhead—not his footsteps but the creaking of roof beams and poles. Dust filtered down from the ceiling, catching the light from the fire and the single lamp. Trish Lovell, who had been dozing in spite of herself, jerked awake.

Staggs was already up, alertly staring at the ceiling. He snatched a rifle from the table and held it ready. Trish watched the movement of his eyes as he tracked the creaking movement above them, starting at the back of the soddy and slowly creeping toward the front of the slanting roof.

The sounds ceased.

Both the woman and her captor waited, hardly breathing. A minute crawled by. Staggs shifted position uneasily, moving to a far corner of the room. His small eyes darted back and forth from the roof where the last surreptitious creaking had been heard to the barred door and shuttered window at the front of the house.

Trish Lovell cleared her throat. "Maybe . . . maybe it wasn't him." Her voice sounded unnatural, strained to a higher pitch than normal. "There are critters sometimes . . . wolves." Once again she thought of the ghost on the ridge the night Garrison arrived.

"It's him," Staggs said harshly. The waiting was drawing his nerves as taut as newly strung wire. "Damn him—"

A small sound made him catch his breath. There followed a sudden commotion directly over the center of the room, a thumping and dragging. In an instant what was happening became clear. A hole appeared. Snow and wind and cold spilled through the opening—the hole Cullen had made where his leg plunged through the roof when it was unable to bear his weight.

Crouching in his corner of the room, Staggs fired once, then two more quick shots. Two of the bullets thudded into ceiling poles. One of these bit off a piece of beam, leaving a white gouge like a bite taken out of an apple. One shot apparently found the opening.

As soon as he had fired, Staggs lunged across the end of the room by the fireplace, as if to escape an answering bullet from the roof.

There was none.

Silence. A thin plume of snow drifted downward through the hole like smoke.

"Garrison? Damn you, Garrison, I'll see you dead and froze!"

Silence answered him. A silence that, as it lengthened into minutes, mocked Staggs' baffled rage.

~ 2 ~

The day had taken its toll on Dave Garrison. The fight with Dandy, the punishing ride on the mare, the search of the barn and the laborious encircling maneuver on foot that had ended with the discovery of the bodies of Ramon Sanudo and Cullen—all had extracted a price from a body already weakened by the effects of a gunshot wound and a growing hunger. They had left Garrison feeling spent, hardly able to move.

For a long time he huddled in the hollowed-out snow cave he had found on the rise behind the Pryor soddy.

While he waited for some strength to return, he had to fight constantly against the temptation to doze. He used snow to wash his face, the cold shocking him awake. He watched Dandy's unhappy mare. She lingered near the barn, her head and neck drooping after a while. When he got back over that way, he thought, maybe he could get her safely into the barn.

His mind circled endlessly around the problem confronting him: how to get Staggs out of the house without endangering Trish Lovell. He found no answer. Staggs was safe where he was. He would be a fool to abandon the walled protection of the soddy.

During his long period of inactivity Garrison was convinced that the hole in his side had stopped bleeding. He wondered how much blood he had lost. Enough to fill a pail, he thought, judging by how heavy Ramon's rifle felt when he lifted it.

His gaze was caught by a hump in the middle of the roof. It marked the area where Cullen's leg had broken through, trapping the big man and enabling Garrison to escape. The opening had been covered over with a buffalo hide weighed down with rocks to hold it in place. After some thoughtful speculation Garrison decided it was time to worry Staggs a little more. If he couldn't be stampeded easily, he might yet be pushed bit by bit toward some reckless action. The waiting was harder on him than on Garrison, who had the patience of an Apache.

He crawled down the slope of the roof, quietly removed the weights that held the frozen hide in place, brushed snow from the covering. Then he waited, listening, knowing that Staggs and the woman in the room below must have heard him.

For a moment lifting the buffalo hide seemed beyond

his strength. Disgusted with this unwonted weakness, he dragged the hide away and stumbled back off the roof. He fell into the snowbank as shots slammed at his ears like three sharp blows.

When Staggs began to yell up at him, Garrison smiled for the first time in a long while.

After another brief rest he left his perch behind the soddy and once more made the long and debilitating journey that eventually brought him behind the barn. His loose plank was still in place. He managed to climb up to the loft as he had before. There he rested again, waiting for dark.

Staggs' voice awakened him. He shook himself, chagrined that he had fallen asleep but grateful that it had happened here, in the comparative shelter of the barn, and not outside in the snow where he would have been exposed to the deeper cold of night. From that sleep he might not have awakened. . . .

He sat up, shaken by a wracking chill. His body ached. The cold seemed to have penetrated to the marrow. He was certain that he had heard Staggs calling out, but now there was only the sound of the wind whistling and sighing softly around the boards of the weathered barn, searching out each crack. Maybe he had only dreamed the harsh rasp of Staggs' voice calling out.

Garrison started to crawl forward toward the edge of the loft. In the darkness one hand slipped through a hole in the floor, brushed a hard surface, scraped across a ragged edge of wood. He knelt, shaking his fingers as if he might shed pain in the way one sheds water from his fingertips.

He remembered seeing that hole the first time he was in the loft. Now he realized that the rest of the loft floor was unexpectedly solid, betraying no softness of rot. That hole seemed oddly placed.

One of the shutters over the loft window remained folded back where Garrison had climbed through. The window traced a long, cool, pale-white shadow across the floor of the loft. The rectangle of dim light fell across the hole in the floor. From the darkness immediately below the opening, something glittered.

Garrison brought his eyes closer to the opening. From one angle he was able to peer through to the floor of the barn below, seeing the broad back of a horse. From another angle that glimpse was cut off. Something was in the way, and from that patch of blackness came the soft metallic gleam.

Garrison reached through the hole, tentatively, probing with his fingers. They traced a rough kind of shelf, wedged against one of the loft's supporting beams. From below, he supposed, it would appear only as additional buttressing for the structure. But in fact there was a shallow shelf only a few inches deep but several feet wide. He could not find one end of it.

A hiding place, he thought, feeling a sharp lift of excitement. He fumbled along the shelf again. This time his fingers brushed against a small object that moved. He seized it, turned it in his fingers unbelievingly, and drew it out. When he held it up in the dim shine from the window opening, light glowed in his fingers.

Garrison stared at the round wafer of gold in his hand.

The possible meaning of his discovery washed away any lingering cobwebs from his brain, leaving him fully awake. He lay flat on the floor and plunged his arm all the way through the opening. He felt along the shelf as far as he could. One end butted against an upright post, which he realized was part of the framing for a stall. He guessed that the same would be true of the other end of the concealed shelf, although he could not reach that far.

He saw more clearly why the shelf was not visible from below. It had been designed to appear as part of the solid framing for the stall.

A place for Virgil Pryor to hide something he did not want found.

The trouble was, along the length of the shelf as far as Garrison could reach, there was nothing to be found. Pryor's treasure had consisted of a single gold coin.

While Garrison considered this, it struck him that his hands, in spite of all his groping, were not dusty or dirty. The shelf was clean. Which meant, of course, that it had recently been used, perhaps its entire surface covered with sacks of gold and silver. From which one coin had spilled and been overlooked when the sacks were removed.

Pryor had changed his mind. He had, finally, been unwilling to gamble that his treasure would not be found in his absence. He must have known that the kind of men who would come hunting for him and his gold were easily capable of tearing down the barn, board by board. The barn and house and anything else that stood. While the possibility remained that he had hidden his hoard elsewhere in the vicinity, it seemed more likely that he had taken it with him.

"Garrison! I know you're out there. You hear, Garrison?"

He climbed down from the loft, shivering uncontrollably, partly from excitement, he supposed—few men were immune to the thrill of discovering gold, however little of the precious metal turned up in the pan—but more from the chill that gripped his body. He crept forward through the darkness of the barn, past the reassuring warmth of the horses, until he was able to peer through a crack at the front of the building toward the house.

A thin vertical bar of light, the height of a man, instantly caught his eye. It defined a narrow opening at the door of the soddy. "Garrison?" Staggs shouted through the crack in the doorway. "I'm givin' you one last chance, you and this yellow-haired lady. Walk out where I can see you, with your hands up high, and I don't put a bullet in her pretty head."

The threat jolted Garrison. The possibility was one that he had been afraid of from the beginning—that Staggs would threaten harm to Pryor's woman as a way of forcing Garrison's hand. The blunt warning was not one he could take lightly, given the feeling of desperation he had been trying to build up in the outlaw.

At the same time, Garrison could not give in to the threat. No promise Staggs might make could be believed. All he wanted was to lure Garrison into the open, into the notch of his gunsight. . . .

He wondered what she would think. That he was abandoning her again? That he was willing to sacrifice her? But he couldn't take those things into account. If he threw in his hand now, she would be even worse off.

He had to find a way to stall. Something that would make Staggs pull back from the edge. But what?

He felt the hardness of the gold coin in his hand.

The gold had brought Staggs here in the first place. The gold had caused Cullen and Dandy to take the big jump. Gold was the one thing that might divert Staggs' attention from the woman.

There was no time to make the long, slow, circuitous trek that would allow him to keep out of Staggs' sight while he reached the rise behind the soddy. And even though it was dark, there was enough starlight to make the snow glimmer softly like pearls. If he tried to cross the yard in the open, Staggs would surely spot him.

At that moment Dandy's piebald drifted between Garrison and the house. The mare stopped close to the barn, pawing at the snow, sensing his presence.

"I'm gonna count ten, Garrison! You want to see this long-haired partner of yours while you'd still want to look at her, throw out your iron where I can see it and foller it real slow. You got ten fingers to count on, drifter! One . . . two . . ."

Staggs began to count slowly, dragging it out. He wasn't sure of his hand, Garrison thought. He might even be pulling a bluff, although that was not a chance Garrison could take.

He slipped out through the front door of the barn and dodged behind the pinto. Grabbing her trailing reins, he clucked at her soothingly. He led her as fast as he could across the yard, swinging around to the right of the soddy's door and away from the window. As soon as he judged that he was out of Staggs' line of sight he dropped the reins and broke into a run. He could hear Staggs counting. "Five! Your time's running out, Garrison! Six . . ."

Garrison went up the slope to the right of the soddy, blundering into deep snow. He struggled out of it, breathing hard, a catch in his side. By luck he stumbled onto a patch of ground blown clear of most of the snow cover. In a few strides he reached the back edge of the soddy's roof.

"Nine!" Staggs shouted angrily. "Ten—"

Garrison reached the hole in the center of the roof and tossed the gold coin through the opening. He heard it strike the table, bounce once and flip to the floor.

Staggs stopped counting.

In the sudden quiet Garrison called out softly. "You

harm her, Staggs, that's the last of that gold you'll ever see. She's the only one knows where the rest of it is buried!"

~ 3 ~

Staggs stared at the gold coin as it spun briefly before it flopped over on its side. His glance, startled and uncertain, lifted toward the hole in the ceiling.

As suspicion flared, his grip on Trish Lovell's arm tightened. He had been holding her in front of him near the door, his six-gun pointing at her head. He shoved her toward the coin, which lay on the floor a few feet in front of the hearth. "Pick it up," he demanded, "and bring it here!"

He watched the ceiling cautiously as she obeyed. If Garrison had been playing a trick, he would be shooting at the wrong target. . . .

Nothing happened. Silently the woman retrieved the coin and handed it to him. He tried to read her expression. A moment earlier, the gun at her head, she had been white and trembling, her eyes despairing. Now she appeared almost . . . happy.

He stared at the gold piece. "How do I know this is what you say?" he demanded, his threat to the woman's life momentarily forgotten. He raised his voice. "One gold piece don't prove nothin'!"

"She gave it to me," Garrison answered him, the voice drifting out of the night, bodiless, no way for Staggs to pinpoint its source. "You know where it came from."

It was true. There had been gold as well as silver in the stolen moneybags. This coin was shiny and new, like many of the others in the sacks. It was true. . . .

He glared at Pryor's woman accusingly, as if outraged

that she had lied to him. "You'll talk now!" he snarled. "You'll tell—"

"You have to kill me first," Garrison taunted him. "Put me under and you'll have it all, Staggs. You won't even have to share it with your pardners now. It's all yours."

In answer Staggs fired at the ceiling, the Colt's six-shooter kicking in his hand until the hammer fell on an empty chamber. He threw the gun down and grabbed his rifle. His eyes stung from the gunsmoke. He felt himself choking on it.

Then he heard the woman coughing. For the first time he realized that the smoke was thick in the room, too thick, spreading wherever he looked. In alarm he stared toward the hearth. A gray mass of smoke billowed toward him. "Douse that fire!" he yelled at the woman. But she seemed not to hear him. She was bent over, coughing and spluttering.

Staggs started toward the water bucket at the end of the hearth. He heard a shot. A bullet smacked into the wooden table less than an arm's length away. Staggs dropped to the floor and rolled frantically away from the table.

At floor level he could breathe more easily, but the smoke was now a thick pall throughout the small soddy. Garrison had stopped up the chimney! The fire had been built up for cooking the evening meal. Staggs himself had thrown more wood onto the fire after he had eaten. The smoke was turning blacker as it thickened. The woman had dropped to the floor nearby, choking.

In sudden rage Staggs rose and lunged at the window. He threw the shutters open and smashed the window with the butt of his rifle. Smoke washed through the opening like water through a break in a dam. But in the act of getting to his feet Staggs had swallowed smoke. He began to choke, unable to breathe. The hot smoke seared his lungs and panic lashed at him.

No drifter could beat him like this! He stumbled to the door, threw it open and burst out of the soddy.

As Staggs whirled toward his tormentor on the roof, Staggs' eyes were blinded by tears. He fired blindly. His rage sought words but his lungs were filled with smoke and the only sound he made was a tortured wheeze.

He never saw Garrison. Staggs felt the brutal impact of lead tearing into his body. The blow spun him around and dropped him to his knees. A wild, wordless protest died in his throat as the next blow came. It flattened him. Then he lay still, blackened by soot and smoke, like a pile of ashes in the snow.

4

Garrison found Trish Lovell lying in the open doorway. He dragged her clear and knelt beside her in the snow, feeling a dread forgotten since his childhood. She did not seem to be breathing. "No," he muttered aloud. Then, hoarsely, "Damn it, no—not you!"

She quivered in his arms, doubled up in a sudden wrenching spasm, and began to cough and struggle for breath. He stared down at her, his heart still pounding, though the feeling now was one of delicious relief rather than panic.

Her face was black. He wiped the soot away from her nose and mouth. Her eyes opened at last, luminous blue in her blackened face. When she saw him holding her, she shuddered and cried out. Her arms went around him, gripping with a strange intensity.

He held her for what seemed a long time, until her body was quiet and she was breathing easily. "I am sorry about the smoke," he told her. "It was the only thing I could think of. It was the only way I could drive him into the open. . . ."

She nodded, still unable to speak.

When the diminishing spasms of coughing had ceased and she was able to sit up—her gaze lighting briefly on Staggs' crumpled shape and then shunting aside—Garrison left her. He climbed once more to the roof of the soddy, where he removed the buffalo hide he had stuffed into the top of the chimney. When he was coming back to her, he fell unexpectedly. There was a feeling of surprise over finding himself all of a heap in the snow. He had trouble rising. Something had happened to his arms and legs, as if all the muscle and fiber had turned to jelly. When he finally managed to get up, he sleep-walked as far as the level ground in front of the soddy before he fell again.

Trish Lovell ran to his side. He was shivering, but his face burned, hot to her touch.

∼ 5 ∼

Inside the soddy there was soot everywhere, and the smell of smoke permeated everything. Not waiting for the air to clear completely she helped Garrison inside and had him lie on the floor close to the doorway. She covered him with a blanket and kept the door open a little, not only to let the smoke out but also to give him cleaner air to breathe.

Hastily she rebuilt the fire. When it was blazing she emptied the water bucket of its contents and filled it with snow. Placed close to the heat of the fire the snow melted quickly, and she gave Garrison water to drink. As the air in the room began to return to normal she worried him over to the wooden chair, which she placed close to the hearth.

His drawn, haggard appearance increased her anxiety. He hardly resembled the man who had appeared at her door only two nights ago. The sight of his blood-soaked shirt and the dirty wrapping over his wound sickened her. The wound would have to be cleansed, the bandaging changed.

"You'd best let me have a look at that side of yours," she said gently. "You'll have to take off your shirt."

"I'll be fine," he mumbled. "Don't know what come over me."

"You're not fine at all. Don't try to tell me you're not hurting."

"Not so bad as long as I keep from laughing."

"Don't be foolish, Mr. Garrison," she scolded. "And don't try to treat me like a child. I'm not the child you knew."

"I wasn't thinking that."

"Then take off your shirt. You might have to take off more'n that. You've been gunshot, Mr. Garrison. You know as well as I do that you can't ignore such a thing."

"I don't know as how it's fitting," Garrison grumbled.

"You won't be the first man I've seen without his shirt," she retorted. Almost instantly she regretted the words, which said more than she had intended. He could see the regret in her eyes and something else as well. Her eyes pleaded with him. It was as if her whole being was quickly gathered up and concentrated within those clear blue centers, and she offered the whole of herself to him, beseeching him to—what? Understand, he thought. Forgive.

Without another word he began to peel off his shirt. She gazed at the bloody bandage around his waist without comment, but she paled at the sight. "I think you'd best lie down, Mr. Garrison," she murmured.

"Might be you should let me handle it myself."

All of a sudden the room seemed to tilt. He felt himself go woozy and light-headed. Then her arms were around him, leading him across the room, guiding, gently urging. "Lie back," she said from somewhere above him, and he wondered how he had gotten from the chair beside the fire to a bed. Her bed? "You've fought three men and won. That's enough to handle in one day."

"Couldn't have done it if Ramon hadn't pitched in."

"Yes . . . he did more than anyone had a right to ask."

"He was a man," Garrison said.

Her fingers were light, deft, purposeful. She bathed the wound first in cold water and went away. It was shallower than she had feared. In a little while she was back, and Garrison winced at the sensation of water hot enough to scald his flesh. The burning pain soon subsided. She applied a clean bandage, firmly prodding him to raise himself up when she had to draw the wrapping around his waist.

Finally she said, "That'll do. Now you must rest."

"I'll be fine in a minute or two." He would just lie there for a little time, he thought, until this heavy weariness eased. He couldn't stay in her bed, of course. Not fitting. Besides, she was another man's woman. . . . The thought almost jerked him fully awake, but in another moment he was sliding back into unconsciousness. He began to shiver uncontrollably, muttering aloud, the words incoherent.

Trish Lovell's distress increased as she watched him. He had been too long out in the cold. Weakened by his gunshot, he had taken a bad chill. She added wood to the fire, but as he continued to shiver and burn at the same time, occasionally talking to himself as he slid into and

out of consciousness, she felt a fierce resolve. She could
not let him go on like this. Not after all he had done, all
he had been through on her behalf. There had been an
awful moment when Staggs had called out to Garrison,
threatening her, and there had been no answer, a moment of despair in which she thought that he had left her
to the mercy of others for a second time. But he had not
deserted her, no more now than he had the other time,
eight years ago. Even then he had only done what he
thought was best.

She slipped out of her dress and, after a moment's hesitation, removed her chemise. Then she crawled into the
narrow bed beside him, pulled the blankets over them,
and huddled against him, her arms around his chest,
bringing to him the only gift she had to offer at that moment, the warmth of her own body.

After a long time his trembling subsided a little. She
continued to lie next to him. A few words he had spoken
came back to her, words torn from him after he had
dragged her from the house, words she had heard as if in
a dream. "No—not you!" She whispered them aloud,
savoring them, repeating them now as her own.

And at last he was quiet. His breathing turned deeper,
slower, relaxed in sleep.

She lay beside him through the night.

CHAPTER 10

~ 1 ~

When Garrison woke he felt the same momentary sense of strangeness that he had experienced two mornings before, a strangeness that came not only from opening his eyes to the plain pole ceiling of an unfamiliar place but also from the instant knowledge that he was not alone. He could never be in a room with her, he thought, without knowing she was there even before he opened his eyes.

He discovered her watching him. "Mornin', Mr. Garrison. You've slept late this time."

Trying to sit up, he moved too quickly. For an instant the room reeled. He dropped back onto an elbow, gasping, becoming aware of the tight bind around his waist that turned out to be a clean bandage. "There's been times I've felt more like digging posts," he managed to say.

Trish Lovell smiled. "You won't be doin' that for a spell. You shouldn't try to do much of anything soon. Except . . ."

He waited a moment when she broke off. There had been consternation in her eyes. "Exc tin' what, ma'am?"

"Nothing. I have a little stew, Mr. Garrison, and some biscuits. I'm sorry I don't have more to offer you. You need to eat to help you get your strength back." The unexplained change was in her voice as well as her eyes.

He wondered what had struck her, what thought had popped into her head.

He found that she had washed out his shirt and dried it before the fire. He put it on slowly, sitting on the edge of the bed. His whole body felt stiff and sore. He was as weak as a foal on its first legs. There was a lightness in his head as well. Otherwise, except for being famished, he supposed he felt as much like shaking a hoof as he deserved.

Breakfast, washed down with strong black coffee, restored him remarkably. By the time he pushed away from the table he felt deceptively normal. Don't give me any cows to tail or posts to plant, he thought, but just let me sit here awhile where it's warm and I'll be bright as a new dollar.

The reminder caused him to ask her about the gold coin he had thrown down through the hole in the roof to unsettle Staggs. "I have it," Trish Lovell said. She retrieved it from the ledge over the hearth. "Do you really think it's part of the money Virgil stole?"

"I reckon so." He explained where and how he had found the coin, and she agreed that Pryor must have hidden his money there for a time. She nodded thoughtfully at Garrison's suggestion that Pryor must have taken the money with him, leaving behind only a single unnoticed coin.

She became pensive then, saying little as she busied herself about the soddy, cleaning up after the meal and taking a broom to the back half of the room where Garrison had slept. He saw that she had done some other sweeping before he awoke, for the soddy seemed remarkably clean even though the smoky smell still lingered inside.

When she went outside to shake out her blankets, he saw the dark depression where Staggs had fallen. Garrison stepped outside. A trough through the snow, flanked along its path by backtracking footsteps, showed how she had dragged the body over to the side of the house with the others. The steps, digging deep and sometimes slewing erratically, also told him how she had struggled.

"He didn't deserve a blanket," Garrison said with laconic humor, although he understood her need to hide the view.

She said nothing. Watching her fold the blankets she had shaken out, he wondered suddenly where she had spent the night. He had a vague memory of warm softness enveloping him, a memory that warmed his cheeks and made him uncomfortable. Surely it was something he had dreamed. . . .

From the doorway he saw her looking up at the ridge above the canyon to the north. When she came inside he knew that she was troubled by something other than Staggs. After a moment she said, "Do you remember the night you came, I said I thought I saw a ghost on that rim? Was it you, Mr. Garrison? You never said."

"It was a wolf," he answered. "I found his tracks the next morning."

"You never came that way?"

Garrison shook his head, puzzled by her questions. "I came from town. Took the trail where it followed the creek along this valley."

She stood near the fire, her back toward him. When she finally spoke again he had to strain to hear her. "I told you once that . . . that Mr. Pryor can be a jealous man. He doesn't like another man even lookin' at me. It's . . . it is just the way he is about anything he . . . anything that belongs to him."

Belongs to him. Garrison stared at her in silence.

"Please understand me, Mr. Garrison. I am grateful to you. I want you to stay until you are fit to ride, but . . .

as soon as you are well enough you must leave this house. Virgil musn't find you here."

"Something has unsettled you."

"Don't ask me how, but . . . I have a *feeling*. You must leave soon, Mr. Garrison. As soon as you can."

"I won't bother you long," he said.

Her face crumpled a little at his tone and she turned aside. An awkwardness settled between them, as palpably distinct as the warmth he had sensed earlier, or the quiet pleasure they had shared during their morning meal. It made the house seem smaller. There was no way they could keep from hearing or looking at each other.

He was wondering if it wasn't time to saddle up and ride when, an hour later, he heard her gasp, a quick sucking in of breath as if she had felt a blow. She was at the broken window, staring out as she often did. This time, when Garrison gazed past her shoulder down the snow-softened reach of the valley, he saw a horse and rider.

They watched the rider grow into recognizable shape, a silhouette black against the white beauty of the land. If he had been more himself, Garrison thought, he would have trusted her intuition more, as he always trusted his own.

～～ 2 ～～

He was a handsome man, tall and straight and supple, with sloping shoulders that conveyed a suggestion of power. His face was reddened, wind-burned, and there was a glint of humor in his eyes. It was easy to see how a woman might be taken with him.

Pryor swung down from the gray gelding he rode with an easy grace. His height was accentuated by a long black coat. He wore black gloves and boots of fine soft leather and a stiff-brimmed Stetson, also black. The clothes might have been those of a preacher or a dude, but in his eyes there was nothing of the tenderfoot or the man of God.

"Mrs. Pryor!" he called out cheerfully. "I see you have not been lonely in my absence."

Watching from the doorway to the soddy, Garrison had to check a reply. The choice of what to say belonged to the woman.

"I have been set upon by three men, Mr. Pryor—partners of yours, they claimed. It is because of Mr. Garrison here"—she turned toward him—"that I am alive to tell of it."

"Mr. Garrison . . ." Pryor nodded toward the lanky man in the doorway. Garrison had the drawn appearance of someone who might have to lean against the wall for support. "I'm obliged to you, if what Mrs. Pryor tells me is true."

"It is true enough about your pardners," Garrison said.

Pryor studied him lazily. There was skepticism in Pryor's look, as if he were asking himself how this lean, weathered man who appeared as if a strong wind would blow him over could have survived a fight with three determined and dangerous men. "These . . . partners. What happened to them?"

"Gone under," Garrison said shortly. "You'll find two of them beside the house under that blanket."

"You'll find Ramon, too," Trish said. "He went up against the big man, the one they called Cullen. They did each other in."

"Ramon—and Cullen?" Pryor whistled softly through his teeth. "That is a fight I'd have given my eye teeth to see."

Trish Lovell trailed behind him nervously as Pryor went to the side of the house and pulled the cover away to examine the dead men. He tossed the blanket carelessly back in place, his face expressionless. "You said there were three men. What of the other one?"

"They called him Dandy," Trish said. "He—"

"You'll find him in a meadow," Garrison said from the doorway. A stubborn impulse had kept him from trailing after Pryor to the side of the house. "On that high ground about a mile or so up yonder."

"I see. Are you sayin' you helped him take his rest there, Mr. Garrison?"

"It was a matter of which one of us was going to go through the gates."

Pryor smiled thinly. "I don't reckon Dandy will be invited through heavenly gates. He was one of the devil's own. You must be hell on wheels yourself, Mr. Garrison, to send him to his chosen place. And Staggs to keep him company."

Garrison said nothing. He was beginning to actively dislike Virgil Pryor. Garrison disliked the preacher's clothes, sleek and brushed, the high polished boots, the gloves of soft leather, the smiling mouth and laughing eyes, the smoothly dripping words. He disliked the anxious nervousness Pryor awakened in Trish Lovell. That most of all . . .

"They were your pardners?"

"We . . . had business together." Pryor's tone closed off the question like shutting a door.

"They were looking for money," the woman blurted out. "They said you stole money that was theirs!"

"And you believed them?" He seemed amused when she became flustered. "But why wouldn't you? I'm sure they were mighty persuasive." He glanced at Garrison again. "I'm in your debt, Mr. Garrison, as I said. But you haven't told me how you came to be in the path of all this trouble. You don't have the look of a man who goes around hunting wildcats."

"Mr. Garrison came to see me," Trish said quickly. "You've heard me speak of him before. You must remember—Mr. Garrison is the man who took me from the Comanches and brought me to Cedar Point. He left me in the care of the first Mrs. Bauer."

"Your rescuer?" The words might have been mocking, but this time Pryor seemed genuinely surprised. "You seem to have a way of being Johnny-on-the-spot where my good wife is concerned, Garrison. No wonder she looks on you with such favor." He paused, confronting Garrison at the soddy's doorway. "You have always been a favorite of hers."

"I only happened along—"

Pryor silenced his awkward explanation with a gloved gesture. "There's no need to say any more, Mr. Garrison. You happened along at a lucky time—not once, but twice. As I said, we're obliged to you. Myself as well as Mrs. Pryor."

Mrs. Pryor, Garrison thought with a grimace, as if the taste of the words were sour on his tongue. He turned aside, as much to hide his expression as to clear the doorway so that the others could come inside.

Pryor entered the house ahead of the woman. He sniffed at the smoky smell that still permeated the room. Trish Lovell explained what had happened, Pryor listening in thoughtful silence. He threw his black coat carelessly over the back of the chair near the hearth, peeled off his gloves, momentarily warmed his hands at the fire. Without turning around he said, "When are you planning on leaving us, Garrison?"

"He—he was wounded in the fighting," Trish said, in her voice that anxiousness that Garrison hated. She was different around this man, Garrison thought glumly. Agitated as a chick that sees the shadow of a wheeling hawk. "Surely we can't send him away until he is well enough."

"I'm sure he can answer for himself." Pryor swung around. "I'm not so sure it would be healthy for you to overstay your welcome, Garrison. I've spoken of our obligation to you for what you've done. Otherwise I can tell you I wouldn't be trading soft words with any man I found alone under my roof with my wife."

Garrison felt a reckless thrust of anger. Pryor had spoken too much of his "obligation." In the West, in the rough company Garrison had kept along the way, a man didn't lean so heavily on words—and he was suspicious of one who did. "You have no cause to think ill of her," he said flatly.

"I'm sure I don't," Pryor answered. "But that don't change the plain facts of the matter." His sudden smile was sunny, warm—the smile that had won her heart, Garrison thought. *All Virgil has to do is grin and wink his eye.* To give such a smile to such a man was a cruel trick of nature. Then Pryor said, "I reckon you're strong enough to sit a horse. Take only what you came with."

Stung by the insult, Garrison let his anger show. Before he could give it words Trish Lovell spoke. "I'm sure Mr. Garrison has no wish to stay, now that you are here and I am safe. His wound was only a shallow one. Isn't that the truth of the matter, Mr. Garrison?"

Her tone was now unexpectedly brisk. The indifference it conveyed cooled his anger like a splash of icy water. It caused him to stare at her in disbelief. She looked away, her eyes on Virgil Pryor. Drinking in the warmth of his smile, Garrison thought bleakly.

When she lifted her face toward his again for just an instant, her manner was bright and confident. But he saw something else in her clear blue eyes, an uneasiness that became an unspoken plea.

He nodded curtly. "I reckon I have no reason to stay longer."

In silence he found his coat, his battered hat, his own rifle. Neither Ramon's nor Staggs' weapons were his to claim.

As Virgil Pryor's woman was not his to claim.

When he was at the door Trish Lovell said, "We'll not forget what you've done."

"My wife has a long memory," Pryor said, and now there was a caustic edge in his voice that he made no attempt to soften. "I'm sure you'll have no reason to come this way again."

For Dave Garrison, a drifter but a proud and stubborn man in his way, it cut against his grain to turn his back on that clear warning and walk away, leaving the threat unchallenged. And leaving behind a woman who had, in two days that seemed now like a lifetime, made his wandering life seem empty, as barren and wasted as the desert at high noon.

But he could do nothing else. He could not deny the silent plea he had read in her eyes.

⚊⚊⚊ 3 ⚊⚊⚊

"Stay inside!" Virgil Pryor snapped, unsmiling.

She had started to follow him from the house. Warned, she hung back, fearful that he might see the longing in her eyes as she watched Garrison ride away.

She parted the homespun cloth she had draped over the broken window. Then, standing well back in the room so that Pryor could not see her from where he was in the yard, she watched Garrison lead his horse from the barn. It was not the horse on which they had traveled together eight years ago, the one he had called Blackie.

This was a chestnut mare. She wondered what had happened to Blackie, of whom she had grown so fond. There had been so many things she and Garrison had not had time to talk about. . . .

He mounted up, glanced once at the soddy and nodded curtly in Pryor's direction. Then Garrison rode around a corner of the barn and was gone. So suddenly she was not prepared for it. She moaned softly, moved by an aching sorrow she had known only once since that morning long ago when she woke to learn that he had left her. She had felt something of the same grief when Emma Bauer died.

This time Garrison had saddled up only because she had begged him to leave—desperately entreated him with her eyes. She knew that he was not indifferent to her— that he might have answered Virgil Pryor's challenge if she had not intervened. She had acted to save his life. She could not have done otherwise, but the awful import of her decision, the sudden vision of empty loveless years stretching before her, filled her with a sense of total desolation.

Her eyes misted over. She turned away from the window. A moment later she heard Virgil Pryor stomp into the house. Even his step was angry. She felt the tension that came into the room with him even without swinging around to face him. There was a long silence, and she knew he was staring at her.

Finally he spoke. "Did he pleasure you last night so much?" His hand seized her shoulder, spun her around. "Let me see those tears!"

"How did you know about last night?" she burst out. As the blood rose dark along her neck and into her cheeks, she realized that he had goaded her into exposing her true emotions. With loathing she said, "You were watching. You've been here all along, watching, waiting to see what happened! You planned it all!"

Virgil Pryor chuckled. "You don't plan good fortune. You take advantage of it when it comes your way, that's all. How could I plan your drifter happening along when he did? I was expecting my good sidekicks, is all. When Garrison stumbled into the middle of them and got caught, I figgered maybe he'd get lucky and account for one of 'em, no more. He did better than anyone could have guessed. Him and Ramon both. You aren't gonna tell me I planned it so's Ramon would show up and lose his knife in Cullen's belly, are you?"

It was the first moment she had known, so clearly and certainly, how much she hated him. Being frightened was something different, something less than this harsh new emotion. "So now it's over," she said in toneless despair. "You got what you wanted. They're all gone, and you have your gold to yourself."

His smile had once captivated her. Now she saw it cold as this Texas winter, cold as her bed would be from this day on. "Not over," he said softly, shaking his head as if he were speaking to a slow-witted child. "There is still the matter of last night's doings in my house."

"Nothing happened!" she cried.

"You forget . . . I was watching."

"Then you know he was hurting. He was sick—he'd taken a chill. I tried to make him comfortable, that's all. Do you think I could do any less when he saved my life?"

"You did more than that, I'm sure. Didn't you make sure that he was warm?" He chuckled when he saw the dark flush touch her cheeks again. "You see, my dear, you can't lie to me. And you must know I can't allow such carryings on—another man pleasuring himself under my own roof with the woman who belongs to me."

"I don't belong to you! I'm not your dear! You never even married—"

He struck her so hard that her senses whirled and her

knees buckled. As she stumbled backward her hip banged against the table. She caught the edge to steady herself. "You belong to me as long as I say you do! I don't need a preacher to tell me what's mine." Pryor grabbed her by the wrist and jerked her toward him savagely. With his free hand he threw the door open. "Now we'll see if we can't tempt your bold Lochinvar to come back to rescue you again. That's what he is to you, isn't he? The sweetheart you'd run away with in a minute, when you're already bespoken to another?"

"No, Virgil, please—let him go! He didn't do anything. He didn't even know. . . ."

He dragged her outside, ignoring her protests. "Let him hear you yell. He's not so far away he won't hear you." He slapped her viciously, holding her with one hand while she struggled to elude the blows that rocked her head back and forth. "Yell! You want him back, don't you? Damn you, woman, *holler!*"

She bit her lip until she tasted blood, stifling the cries that welled up in her throat. A heavy blow dropped her to her knees. Seeing her stubborn resistance, Pryor suddenly dug his fingers into her long hair. He wrapped it around his wrist with a quick twist and jerked upward with all his strength.

An involuntary shriek came before she could choke it off. She set her teeth against the pain as he began to drag her across the yard by her golden hair. She prayed that Garrison had not heard her scream.

$\sim$ 4 $\sim$

Garrison struck eastward along the valley, resisting the impulse to look back. No good came of looking back. He rode in the sullen mood of a cowhand looking around for a dog to kick, angry with himself, with Virgil Pryor, with Trish Lovell. What made her stand by a man like Pryor? How could she remain blind to what he was?

Garrison had known women who had stayed with men for motives too obscure to understand—for what seemed little more reason than a willingness to absorb blows, verbal abuse, treatment you would think would drive any woman over the border. They stayed, as a dog, with unfathomable loyalty, will continue to follow a bad-tempered owner who offers it only cuffs and kicks in return for its slavish affection. Garrison had never expected the feisty girl he had rescued from the Comanches to grow up to be so meek and lacking in self-respect.

Maybe she simply felt that she had given her pledge, her word, even without benefit of a formal ceremony, he thought, trying to justify her. She was stubborn—had been even as a child. She would not give up easily on anything she had sworn to do. . . .

Each explanation came up short. Something was missing.

She was afraid.

Garrison slowed the eager chestnut's pace—cooped up for two days, the horse was full of vinegar—and came almost to a stop. Had she acted only out of fear?

While he hesitated, growling to the chestnut to be patient, Garrison's eye was caught by something off to his left that disturbed the tranquil purity of new snow. The frozen stream had had its coating of ice and snow recently broken. The track emerging on the near side of the stream was that of a single horse and rider. Beyond the stream, where the land rose sharply in steep-walled bluffs, the tracks seemed to end at the foot of these heights. As Garrison studied the bluffs more closely, the tracks reappeared. They followed a natural trail upward.

Those tracks were fresh. And the only man who could have made them was Virgil Pryor.

Acting on a sudden hunch, Garrison turned the chestnut's head and followed the tracks across the stream. The trail, even as it climbed, was easy to follow. A well-used animal path that would be familiar to anyone living on this land. In minutes it brought him to the relatively flat top of a mesa. To the west it rose gently like the swell of a long wave, cresting at the rim that marked the near side of the canyon into which Garrison had plunged. The tracks he followed turned toward that rim, falling into line with other sign. This trail had been busy, Garrison mused, although the overlapping tracks could have been made by the same horse coming and going many times.

He swung the chestnut along the fresh trail, knowing that it must end at the top of the ridge overlooking Pryor's ranch. Pryor had scouted the scene before riding in. That seemed natural enough in a man with reason to expect trouble. Still, it was clear that this morning wasn't the first time Pryor had ridden this way. How long had he known Garrison was there?

Garrison remembered the night of his arrival, Trish Lovell mistaking him for a ghost she had seen on this same ridge—a ghost or a wolf. He remembered his own sense of something amiss the next morning, a prickly sensation of being watched. The wolf tracks he had found near the barn had banished his unease. Later, the appearance of Staggs and the others had made him forget about Trish's ghost until she mentioned it again this morning.

How long had Pryor been watching?

In that moment Garrison heard a thin, sharp cry. He stiffened. The sound might have been the squeak of some small critter caught in hungry jaws. It was not repeated. But as he listened Garrison felt a chill crawl up his spine until it raised the hairs at the back of his neck.

He plunged forward recklessly. A moment later, dangerously close to the rim of the bluffs north of the ranch buildings, he pulled up. From the edge he stared down at the barn, the snug little soddy with its curl of smoke, the open yard between.

In the middle of the yard Virgil Pryor dragged Trish Lovell by the hair across the open space. She made no sound. In its silence the scene became more brutal.

Garrison shook with anger. In that one flashing glimpse he understood everything. The game Pryor had played these past few days. Trish's refusal to cry out against the pain being inflicted on her. Her desperate appeal to Garrison to leave. She had guessed that Pryor was nearby. She was not afraid of pain, not fearful for herself. She was afraid for *him*.

But Pryor *wanted* him to turn back. A dozen feet from the barn Pryor stopped. He jerked at Trish's hair so hard, trying to force another scream from her throat, that he lifted her off the ground.

Garrison hauled his rifle from its scabbard and, not taking time to aim, loosed a bullet high over the heads of the two small figures far below. He dared not try to aim closer while the two struggled together. "Woman fighter!" he raged, not knowing if he was too far away to be heard. "Yellow-bellied, sand-backed, double-crossing thief! You hear me, Pryor? I'm comin' for you!"

He fired off another shot, still aiming high, and had the satisfaction of seeing Virgil Pryor release the woman and dive out of sight behind the cover of a corner of the barn.

~~~ 5 ~~~

Virgil Pryor crouched low, hugging the front wall of the barn just around the corner. He edged out far enough to peer with one eye at the bluffs east of the canyon.

Without taking his eye from the rim he spoke to Trish Lovell in harsh tones of command. "Fetch me my rifle—the Winchester! It's on the pegs just inside the door."

When he realized she had not moved, he turned his head. The woman stared back at him.

After a moment he said, more gently, "You're right, I shouldn't ought to have hit you." He permitted himself a small smile. "Hell, you know how I get riled, hon', when any other man even looks cross-eyed at you. You're not gonna hold that against me."

"I won't help you kill him."

"Damn it, Trish—!" He caught himself. Garrison had disappeared. Was he still up there on the ridge or had he started back to the winding track that would bring him down to the valley floor? That would take him five minutes, maybe more. If he tried to come down too fast Pryor could simply go over and count the pieces. He had picked his way down that narrow trail himself within the hour. It was slick, treacherous footing.

But Garrison wouldn't fall. Pryor wasn't going to make the mistake both Dandy and Staggs had made of underestimating the drifter.

Pryor ought to be able to see Garrison almost any minute. That descending track was maybe a half mile downvalley—too far for a reliable shot even with a rifle but close enough that movement along the face of the bluffs should be visible. He would know when Garrison was descending.

Pryor scowled. He didn't like uncertainty. He feared no man he could see in front of him, but he didn't like not knowing where Garrison was.

"Trish, bring me that rifle. He won't shoot at you even if he's still waiting up on that rim. Anyways, I don't think he's up there now. He'll be coming down any minute."

He had made a bad mistake, leaving the house without the Winchester. If Garrison learned that and was smart enough, he would avoid a meeting at close quarters where a six-gun spoke with more authority.

"I . . . I can't do that."

She had risen to her feet. She dusted some of the snow from her long skirt. She spoke quietly, without bravado, a decision made. Pryor had to hide his rage. She would pay dearly for this stubbornness. He wouldn't forget.

He risked another quick look down the valley. No shot came from the nearby rim. He ventured a longer scrutiny, his gaze quartering the bluffs at a point where he judged the trail to be. There was no sign of Garrison yet. But he *had* to come that way.

Glancing up again at the rim above the canyon, Pryor wondered why Garrison had shot so high. Two shots, neither of them close. Because he had misaimed? It was natural to shoot high when you were firing on a downward line across any considerable distance, but Garrison should have corrected on his second shot. Or had he deliberately aimed high because he was afraid of hitting Trish?

The speculation deepened Pryor's scowl. He knew that he would not have hesitated.

Trish was still watching him from the middle of the yard. "If I have to go after that rifle myself," Pryor said evenly, "it isn't somethin' I'll be likely to forget." Time to stop coddling her, he thought. She was afraid of him— had good reason to be. "I want it *now*."

She nodded then, her expression unreadable, contained. She turned and walked slowly over to the door of the soddy. Pryor checked his exasperation at her methodical pace. Good enough, she was doing what she was told. There would be time to reason with her later about the need to jump when he gave an order. Even a steady horse had to be reminded once in a while who was boss. And you had to know when to use the whip and when to offer a cube of sugar.

She walked into the house without looking back at him. The door closed behind her.

Pryor heard the bar drop into place over the door.

He felt the jarring thud of the bar in his body, flinching, instinct understanding what she had done before his mind grasped the truth. She wasn't obeying his command. She hadn't gone to get the rifle he had asked for. She was locking him out of the house.

Pryor's rage exploded. He came out of his crouch on a run, barreling across the yard. The door might be barred but not the broken window. Even if she tried to close the shutters, they weren't strong enough to keep him out.

Halfway across the yard he saw movement behind the makeshift curtains over the window, a glimpse of her face where the cloth parted, then the hard gray glint of metal as the barrel of a rifle poked over the sill like a tongue of steel. He was still on the run when he saw the spurt of flame, heard the slam of the rifle firing.

Shock. He stumbled to a stop, quivering with fear, hating the thudding in his chest, the cold, sliding clutch of panic in his gut. The bullet had dug into the ground close enough to make him dance. Now the muzzle tipped upward. It centered on his chest.

Stunned, he couldn't move. "Trish! My God, woman, this is Virgil. Your own—"

"Don't come a step closer! Not one step."

"You don't know what you're doing!"

"I know exactly what I'm doing. The only thing I don't understand is why I didn't put the first bullet into you. I didn't miss—I only aimed to stop you. But if you try to come any closer, I'll cut you down. You better believe me, Virgil Pryor."

He believed her. It was incredible, impossible, but he believed. "Throw out a rifle," he said. It was no longer a command. Now he was *asking*.

"You wanted to fight him so bad, do it with what you have."

"That's no fair fight!" He was uneasily aware of time lost, of events slipping out of his control. "He's got a rifle. That's no fair fight in the open when I've only got this Colt." His hand moved.

"Don't try it, Virgil. Don't tempt me. You can't see me well enough to kill me with one shot. And I swear I'll drop you where you are if you try."

His right hand hovered over the butt of his Colt, the temptation to draw held back on a hair trigger of self-control. But she meant what she said, he knew. And he couldn't risk a blind shot through the curtained window.

He swung around and stalked away, breaking into a run toward the barn. He was only a few steps from the barn door when the rifle cracked again. He heard the bullet bite into the wall of the barn just above the door. She had aimed high this time, perhaps unwilling to risk hitting any of the horses inside the building. That realization caused him to chance another step. Her third shot fanned his cheek.

"You wanted this fight!" she cried. There was an edge of wildness in her voice that terrified him, for it convinced him at last that he had lost all control over her and she was capable of anything. "Stay out in the open. He's comin' now. He's comin' after you, Virgil!"

And she fired again, this time at his feet, forcing him away from the barn door and over toward the side. Another shot herded him past the corner of the barn into the open.

And he saw Garrison riding headlong up the valley toward him. A hundred yards or less away, coming fast. Pryor drew his Colt. He didn't like this—didn't like it at all. He didn't like having Trish Lovell behind him with a rifle aimed at his back. He didn't like the way the drifter

was coming straight at him. His chestnut horse was running hard along a trail already broken through the snow.
Garrison was bent low; he offered no real target at all.

Pryor snapped off two quick shots—not at the small,
bobbing target of the rider but at the larger target
offered to him. The horse stumbled. Garrison tried to
hold her head up but her gait broke and she went down.
He somersaulted over her head. Pryor felt a leap of exul-
tation in his chest when he saw Garrison's rifle fly out of
his hand to land ten yards beyond him in the snow.

Even as Garrison hit the ground and rolled, Virgil
Pryor started toward him on the run. He had covered ten
yards before he whirled, dropped to one side and fired at
the window of the soddy. He had no real hope of hitting
an invisible target there but he meant to drive her from
the window. He jumped to his feet again and turned toward the fallen rider in triumph.

The prickling fear that had made him fire at the
woman in the house had kept him from watching long
enough to be sure that Garrison was down. When he
swung around Garrison was on his knees, thirty yards
away. His six-gun was in his hand. Pryor felt a jolt of
surprise like a knee in the small of the back. Then Garrison fired.

There was only one thought in Pryor's mind as
pain struck: *It was her doing.*

Then, like Garrison, he was on his knees in the snow.
The two men faced each other like penitents. But Garrison still had his gun in his hand and Pryor had somehow
dropped his own Colt. He tried to reach for it. There was
another shot, the sound oddly thin and brittle. Pain hit
again. For an instant it expanded in him like a ball of
needles. Then it was gone and there was nothing, nothing
at all.

~~~ 6 ~~~

"I couldn't shoot him down!" Trish Lovell sobbed. "I wanted to but I couldn't do it."

"It's all right. You did fine."

"No, no—I should have! You might have been killed—"

"I wasn't, and it's done now. It's over."

"He's been here all along, he told me so. He let those other men do whatever they wanted with you—with me. He didn't care!"

"I figgered that out," Garrison said.

The words kept tumbling out of her as he led her back into the house—the fears, the anxieties, the questions, the regrets. He answered her questions with any words that came to him, soothing her with the sounds of them more than anything else. He held her when she started to shake.

She shuddered when she told of seeing him fall from his horse. "I thought he'd shot you. I wanted to die myself."

Garrison assured her that a tumble in the snow never hurt anyone. Even his chestnut mare was unhurt. One of Pryor's shots had missed, the other had only creased her shoulder, just enough to break her stride.

"I'm surprised you can even stand up," she said, suddenly calm, her blue eyes grave. "I'll never forgive myself for sending you away like that."

Garrison grinned, a long, slow grin that spread across his face about as fast as the sun rising. "I'll remind you of that. Every year or so, in case you start to forget."

That stopped her short. She stared at him. "You didn't have to go," she said. "Just because I told you—" She broke off, and smiled back. "All right . . . but only once a year. A woman shouldn't be made to feel guilty more than that for being wrong once."

"That's fair enough," Garrison answered.

It was strange to talk of years when he had always thought of days and nights, this day and this night, just drifting along from one to the next, worrying about the future no more often than he worried about which way the wind might blow. Strange and a little unsettling, but Garrison knew that this moment, this woman smiling up at him, had touched something deep within him that had been waiting to find its place.

This place.